SOLD

TO THE

SHEIKH

CHLOE COX

ISBN: 1480153443
ISBN-13: 978-1480153448

DEDICATION

To anyone who ever gave me a book as a child: thank you.

CONTENTS

SOLD TO THE SHEIKH

Dear Reader,

I have a whole lot of fun writing all my erotic romances, but the story of Sheikh Bashir and Stella Spencer is especially close to my heart. This book is for everyone who has been able to put the pieces of a broken heart back together and try again, and it's especially for anyone who is still looking for the strength to do so.

But, that said...I feel like I have to warn you! Sheikh Bashir and Stella get up to some crazy sexual shenanigans, and I wouldn't want anyone to go ahead and, um, try anything out without doing a lot of research. In particular, the thing at the end of Chapter 9...

Don't try that at home. Not as, like, an impromptu thing. And not without a lot of practice, patience, the proper accoutrements, and a partner you trust!

Wishing you lots of love and happiness...
Chloe

CHAPTER 1

Stella Spencer stared at her tear-streaked face in the mirror and told herself to suck it up.

This is pathetic, she thought. *And it's unprofessional. Nobody wants to see a crying woman at a sex club.*

Well, no one she cared to meet, anyway. She tried not to judge some of the things that went on at Club Volare NY, but sometimes she needed to remind herself that everything that happened at the club was always strictly consensual. There'd been a few scenes that could've fooled her, but then, Stella didn't pretend to be totally fluent in the complicated language of human sexuality.

Which was why it had been such a surprise when they hired her. It had been a gift, really, given Stella's circumstances. Lola Theroux had just sort of appeared out of the past at a college alumni event, zeroed in on her old, forgotten friend, and offered her a mysterious "position" at an exclusive "club." If Lola noticed that the alumni mixer was the first time Stella had managed to get out of the house in months, or that she'd looked wan and harried and not quite put together, she didn't seem to mind. Or maybe she'd just been too polite to comment. The divorce had, of course, made the damn society pages. Stella was convinced that *everyone* noticed.

But Club Volare was a reason to get out of the house. At Club Volare, she could be someone else. She hadn't run into anyone from her old life. Her ex-husband might be wealthy, but he wasn't quite Volare-wealthy.

So why am I freaking losing it today?

One of those questions without an answer. But it didn't matter; Stella had to get back out there and host. She had a job to do. She rummaged through her purse, looking for an eyeliner pencil. She was pretty sure raccoon eyes wouldn't do.

"Stella?"

Stella nearly put her eye out. She would never get used to the silent swiveling doors that were a Volare trademark. It was like Catie had appeared out of nowhere.

"I'll be right back out—just reapplying." Stella tried to smile. "Can you cover if there's no one up at the front?"

Catie's expression probably should have warned Stella about what was coming. The young courtesan-in-training leaned back against the open door with a sly grin and said, "It's not that. Mistress Lola wants you in the Pearl Room."

The Pearl Room. Stella was not a fan of the Pearl Room. Each of the little sections in Club Volare had their own vibe, and the Pearl Room was full of flashy European glamour and women who were so beautiful you couldn't be sure that they were actually human. If you were having a fat day, the Pearl Room was not where you'd go to feel better. And Stella felt like she'd been having a fat day for the past few months.

Not fat, she reminded herself. *Curvy. Healthy. Totally normal.* Six months ago, this wouldn't even have crossed Stella's mind, but six months ago, she hadn't been dumped. And anyone would look a little *zofteig* compared to the sorts of people who hung out in the Pearl Room.

Stella hurried along, smoothing down her black dress, wishing it weren't quite so form-fitting, and decided she'd take her usual detour via the back stairs. Club Volare leased the top few floors of an expensive boutique hotel, and there were several sets of stairs and elevators for staff use only. She could use one of those to sneak up to the unobtrusive side door embedded in a wall of the Pearl Room and slip in without having to run a gauntlet of judgy models.

She did, however, pause to adjust her boobs a little higher in her tight dress. *Might as well work what you've got.*

Stella took a deep breath, closed her eyes, and leaned into the hidden door, hoping to open it as silently as possible.

"What the hell?" said an irate, female voice.

Oh shit. Stella had felt a bump against the door, and heard the tell-tale clatter of high heels. She'd definitely just nailed some model who'd been standing next to the door. She slipped inside expecting to find a pissed off glamour girl in need of an apology, but was instead blinded by a very bright light.

"Ok, *what* is going on?" Stella said, still trying to get her bearings. Even with her hand covering her eyes, she could barely make out a bunch of long, elegant female bodies, all lined up against the wall that she'd hoped to sneak past unnoticed. So much for that plan.

"Who is this?"

That was definitely a male voice. Deep. Sharp. Accented. It seemed to hang in the air, and reverberated through Stella's body in a very distracting way, so that it took her a moment to realize that she'd obviously interrupted a Club scene of some sort. That was *not* done.

Not good.

"Close the door behind you, Stella, and face forward." Stella still couldn't see a thing, but she recognized that as the voice of her friend, Lola, but not as she knew her—not exactly. This was the commanding voice of Mistress Lola of Club Volare, and Stella obeyed before she even realized what was happening.

Stella blushed. She wasn't some sort of simpering servant, and her unthinking obedience made her feel somehow very vulnerable.

She put her hand back over her eyes, trying to orient herself, but still couldn't see squat. "Sorry, I didn't mean to—"

"Take your hand away from your face."

That male voice again; this time, harsh. And...dominating.

"*Excuse* me?" Stella said.

"Remove your hand," the voice said. The suggestion of a smile played around the edge of his words. "I want to see your face."

Stella's first instinct was to tell Commandant Whoever He Was to get bent, but something in his tone gave her pause. He wanted to see her face. He'd already seen the rest of her, plain as day in the middle of whatever light they had trained on her, plump and short compared to the women on either side of her, and stuffed into an ill-fitting black dress. It had been a long time since she'd felt like any man really saw her, let alone wanted to see more of her. And the harsh, commanding man wanted to see her face.

She removed her hand and said, "I'll show you mine if you show me yours."

Oh, great joke, Stella. Hilarious.

The man ignored her. "Please adjust the light, Lola," he said.

The light clicked downward so it was no longer directly in Stella's eyes, but upon her breasts. Stella tried not to think about that. She hadn't realized she was squinting, but now her face relaxed. She could make out a few figures, one she took to be Lola, and another, a man, a tall, broad silhouette, standing next to her friend. *Why am I just standing here like a dumb prop?* she thought. She felt like some sort of specimen, pinned to the wall by a spotlight. This was not her. Not how she thought of herself. And she didn't want to think about how she looked compared to all the other women on display.

"Ok, yes, very funny," she said. "Obviously I've interrupted something. Lola, is there something—"

"That is the one that I want," the man said abruptly. "Make the arrangements."

And the tall, shadowy figure disappeared behind the light.

~ ~ ~

"No," Stella said, swishing fruitlessly at the air with her hand. "No, no, no."

Lola only smiled. Her silence was infuriating, and still Stella felt compelled to fill it.

"You *know* this isn't my thing, Lola. You know I'm not cut out for it. I don't...look, I'm not judging, one way or the other, but I don't get the whole BDSM thing. Or Dom/sub thing, or whatever. See? I don't even know what to call it."

"You're doing fine so far," Lola said. She leaned back in her chair, head nestled in a pile of rich auburn hair, and this time her smile spread across her whole face. She looked like Stella's friend again.

"But I don't think I can do this," Stella said. "It's just not me."

"Are you sure? Sometimes others can see what we hide from ourselves."

Stella looked at her. "Don't try that fortune cookie Volare-type philosophical crap on me."

"Hmm. Deflection," Lola said. "Interesting. I doubt he'll put up with that."

Stella threw her hands up in frustration. "Who?"

A buzzer sounded, emanating from the always-locked door that led to Lola's plush office space. Stella had always wondered about her friend's choice in decor; lots of comfortable looking black velvet and leather that somehow managed to make Stella feel transgressive, even if she wasn't doing anything wrong. And right now she felt as though she were definitely doing something wrong. She looked at Lola, alarmed.

"Him," Lola said with a smile, and reached across her desk to buzz someone in.

Stella was too embarrassed to turn around, even as footsteps approached. She stared wildly at Lola instead, making crazy eyes, hoping her friend would come to her senses and call off this obvious, *obvious* mistake.

But Lola had on her game face now, impassive and stern. She had become Mistress Lola.

Stella swallowed and took a breath, determined to turn and face whoever was behind that imperious voice, but she didn't have a chance. A hand on the small of her back, another at her chin, and suddenly she was turned towards a broad figure, looking up directly into a set of hard black eyes.

"Tell me your name," the man demanded. It was the same booming voice, but now it was attached to a luminous, coffee-colored face. He had beautiful skin smoothed out over a set of rough-hewn, masculine features: a heavy brow, a Roman-looking nose, and a strong, hard chin. Only his lips looked soft.

His eyes narrowed. "I said: tell me your name."

She said immediately, "Stella Spencer."

Stella had never heard herself sound so small. It was infuriating. Why had she answered him? This man, with the voice, and the face chiseled from beautiful rock, and the dark, hypnotizing eyes—this man was staring directly into her. He was holding her face, pressing her close to him, where she could feel the entire hot, hard length of his body. It felt like a small miracle that she could remember words at all. If she could only get out a few words, why didn't she use them to stand up for herself, and tell him to back off?

Why didn't she want to?

"Stella," he said slowly, as though rolling it around on his tongue to get a feel for it.

And, just as suddenly, he released her. It was like the sun going behind a cloud. He turned and faced Lola instead.

"Is the paperwork complete?" he said.

Lola pushed forward a set of papers on her desk. "Not quite," she said.

He scowled. "What is the difficulty?"

Stella, trying not to flush, forced herself to find her voice. This was ridiculous; the two of them talking like she wasn't even there. She said, "Um, the difficulty is that there's been a mistake, Mr...?"

Slowly, he turned to look at her. His gaze

was intense, total, and completely unnerving. The silence alone was almost unbearable.

"You may address me as Sheikh Bashir," he finally said. "There has been no mistake."

"Yes, there *has*," Stella said, hating herself for getting so flustered. She could still feel the heat of him where he'd touched her. "I wasn't supposed to be there like that. I just barged in. I understand that I interrupted your scene, and for that I apologize. It was completely my fault, and totally inexcusable. I really, really am sorry, but it was an honest mistake."

Sheikh Bashir seemed unimpressed. He registered no expression. It was almost as though Stella hadn't spoken. How could she say this without offending this god-like...*Sheikh?*

Wait, he's really a Sheikh? That's an actual thing?

"I'm not..." she said, struggling to find the words, "Look, I'm not one of the Volare. I'm sorry. It's a mistake."

The Sheikh's nostrils flared, and he turned on Lola, his massive hand falling on her desk.

"She may not be a member of the Volare," he said to Lola, "but there was no mistake."

He grabbed the sheaf of papers, and turned that gaze back to Stella. It was worse than being under a spotlight, she thought. She felt totally bare.

"In this country," he said, his voice tense,

"at this time, I cannot purchase you outright. You will sign an agreement." He turned again to Lola, who wore the mask of a professional. "*She* is the one that I want. Double the fee."

"Ok, seriously, this is ridiculous. I don't know how to make this any clearer. I am not—" Stella began, but the Sheikh turned that stare back on her, and suddenly she lost her train of thought. His eyes flashed, and Stella had the distinct feeling that he was restraining himself. From...something.

When he spoke, his tone left no room for doubt.

"Do not feign outrage with me, Stella Spencer. I have little tolerance for pretension or dishonesty, as you will learn. I do not care who you think you are, or what you are determined to represent yourself to be. The fact is that you have turned your breasts towards me; your nipples are pert, even though this room is quite warm, and your pupils are dilated. You will sign the papers because you want to sign them, and you will present yourself to me in the room I have rented for this purpose, and you will do it now."

And with that, Sheikh Bashir threw the papers on the desk and strode out of the room.

It was a moment before Stella could speak. It took her a few seconds to even realize that her mouth was open. Eventually, she turned toward her old friend.

"I'm giving you the long weekend off," Lola said.

"Lola," she managed, but it sounded desperate, rather than angry.

"It's fifty thousand dollars for the holiday weekend, Stella. Standard safeword arrangement, terminating the contract at a prorated rate. It will change your life," Lola said, and her face softened. "And I'm not just talking about the money."

Stella blinked. *Fifty thousand dollars?*

She thought about how she couldn't even pay the taxes on the ridiculous apartment she'd been awarded in the quickie divorce settlement. She thought about the many empty rooms of that expensive apartment, all of them mocking the memory of the life she thought she'd had with her Robert before he'd dumped her. She thought about the pitying looks she'd gotten from people she might have described, once, as their "mutual friends," and how now those people all made her feel like a pathetic, boring castoff. She thought about her totally barren social calendar.

She thought about how shocking and immediate the Sheikh's touch had been, reminding her that she was, in fact, a woman. It had been like a single frame of color in a black and white movie, like something you didn't even know you were missing until someone showed you that it existed. Here was a man who actually wanted her.

All in a rush, before she could change her mind or the Sheikh could come to his senses, Stella Spencer signed the papers.

CHAPTER 2

Sheikh Bashir al Aziz bin Said was not, generally speaking, an impulsive man. He was a passionate man, of course, but always controlled. Always, supremely, controlled.

And yet he'd just been knocked senseless by this Stella Spencer. He had no idea how it had happened. It simply did not make sense.

This was supposed to be his last hurrah, so to speak, a final extravagance before settling down to duty. Bashir had given up on finding a worthy match for himself, even at Club Volare, and was resigned to a lonely marriage and a lonely life, if it meant serving his country's interests. There were far worse things in the world, Bashir knew. Still, he'd decided to indulge himself with one last holiday at Club Volare, where he might pretend for a little while before returning to the hard realities of life. He was prepared for that. But then, at the last possible moment, there was this Stella Spencer.

He had not been prepared for Stella Spencer. She'd stumbled in with such unassuming beauty and authenticity, and then she appeared to actually challenge him.

He suspected that she challenged everyone, in a way, perhaps without realizing it. So on her guard. So protected, even while unable to hide that authenticity. He'd never forget the way she raised her eyebrow when she'd said, '*Excuse* me?' Such a simple gesture, nothing obviously remarkable about it, and yet, somehow, it drew him in.

He'd laughed. *No one* spoke to him like that. And from the moment he saw her, he'd felt...

He'd been trying to put it into words. In fact, he *had* to be able to put it into words—to name it, to own it—before she arrived for his standard submissive evaluation. Otherwise he had very little hope of staying in control, and the only thing a man in Bashir's position couldn't afford was to lose control with a woman. Especially one like Ms. Spencer.

There was a hesitant knock at the door.

His time was up.

"Enter," he said.

Stella opened the door just wide enough to slip through and closed it quickly behind her, as though she were afraid that someone might notice. She stood very close to the door, keeping her hands on the handle behind her while her chest moved up and down with rapid little breaths. Her large breasts were still pressed high and tight by that sleek dress that only accentuated all of her delicious curves. The flush that had started to spread across her skin in Lola's office had only intensified.

"So...hi," she said, and gave an awkward little wave.

Why was that so endearing? Why was her obvious bumbling—her determination in the face of such social ignorance—attractive? It was like he'd been possessed. Bashir breathed deeply and counted to three.

"Come here," he said, and beckoned for her to stand before him. The room was luxurious—if simple—compared to his luxury suite downstairs. Bashir found the sofa on which he sat to be quite comfortable, the bar was well stocked, and the bed, over on the other side of the room, was large. Stella glanced over at it nervously.

"We won't have need of that quite yet," he said, and her creamy shoulders seemed to relax a little.

Good. Bashir didn't want her frightened. He wanted her overcome. These evaluations had a purpose. He wanted to find out what made her tick, what turned her on, what turned her off. He'd always delighted in putting subs through the best scenes of their lives, but something about Stella Spencer suggested there might be more to it this time.

He watched as she walked slowly forward until she stood a few feet in front of where he sat, and he tried his damnedest to figure out what it was about her. She wasn't particularly graceful, she didn't have the studied allure of most of the Volare women, and yet...and *yet*...

"You wanted me to present myself," she said, and then frowned, apparently embarrassed by such an inane statement. Or perhaps she disliked the phrase itself, with all its implications. Bashir was intrigued when, a second later, she looked into his eyes with an air of defiance. Of pride.

Best to be absolutely clear, then.

"You haven't presented yourself yet, Stella," he said. "Take off your dress."

She flinched. Her face was as open to him as it had been in Lola's office, as it had been in the Pearl Room. Perhaps this was what drew him to her, these flashes of openness, of intimacy. Now he watched her cycle through disbelief, her mind churning behind those blue eyes, and run up against...desire. Her face was a mask of confusion. She needed his help.

"I said: take off your dress, Stella. *Now*."

~ ~ ~

Sheikh Bashir's voice filled the room like a thunderclap, penetrating Stella's mind with the sudden violence of a force of nature and compelling her to act. She very nearly actually *did* it. She'd nearly taken off her dress just because he'd told her to. She came back to herself, her thumbs already hooked under the straps of her dress, and blinked.

What the hell was that? She'd never felt so weak. *I have my safeword. I can always say the safeword.*

Somehow, that didn't help. She didn't fear Sheikh Bashir, even as he arose from the couch with a lazy, predatory grace. She feared her own apparent loss of self-control. What kind of person nearly undresses just because some guy with the voice of God tells her to? What was happening to her?

"I'm sorry," she said, "I told you I'm not...I'm not familiar with these kinds of things. I'm sorry. I think this was mistake, Sheikh Bashir, I really do."

"I grow weary of hearing you say that, Ms. Spencer," he said, and a wry smile played across those soft lips. "It's almost as if you do not trust my judgment."

Stella knew there was something wrong with that argument, but she was having trouble thinking logically. The Sheikh had risen to his full height and had removed his tailored grey suit jacket, tossing it carelessly on the sofa. What was left was an obvious wall of hard muscle under a fitted white, collared shirt, which was tucked crisply into a pair of grey suit slacks.

Maybe he plays polo, Stella thought weakly. She could see the Sheikh fiercely driving a horse around a pitch. *Oh God, what an idiotic thing to think about! You don't know anything about polo! Get a hold of yourself, Spencer.*

But she was frozen to the spot, as though if she stayed perfectly still, maybe Sheikh Bashir would just forget about her. Instead, he came very, very close. Stella remembered the heat of his body from when he'd grabbed her, only a few moments ago in Lola's office, and looked furiously at the floor.

He said, "But it is more offensive to me that you seem to expect *me* not to trust my own judgment, too." He reached out and touched the side of her cheek with the back of his hand. "I know what I see before me. You make it quite plain."

Suddenly, Stella was furious. She'd been torturing herself nightly over what other people must see when they looked at her, what led them to treat her the way that they did, and this stranger had the temerity to just…announce that he knew? Better than she did?

"Oh, *really*?" Stella said, and let the sarcasm fly. She finally looked up to see that he was still smiling. "You think you know me better than I know myself?"

"Apparently."

Stella was not prepared for that.

"But perhaps you need to be convinced," the Sheikh continued, and stepped quickly behind her, resting his large hands on her shoulders. Stella was afraid to move. Not because of what might happen, but because she might miss the feel of him behind her, and she wasn't quite ready for that, either.

Maybe that's the problem, Stella thought to herself. *I've been so afraid of what might happen, I've stopped moving.* She felt something inside twist, and the kaleidoscope of jumbled emotions that she'd become accustomed to carrying around with her fell into a kind of focus. The picture didn't make sense, exactly, but it was a picture now. She *was* afraid. She *had* stopped moving. She'd been hiding.

And this stranger could see that.

If it hadn't been for his warm hands massaging her shoulders, Stella was certain she would've begun to shake. She wasn't sure she could handle whatever he had planned.

"Who do you think you are," she said, and she could not keep the tremble out of her voice, "to talk to people this way?"

The Sheikh's big hands spun her around easily, and he caught her around the waist with his iron arm. His other hand moved upward to cradle her face—and to make sure she looked at him while he spoke to her.

"I am Sheikh Bashir al Aziz bin Said of Ras al Manas," he said with unerring calm, "though that has little to do with my ability to talk to you this way, or my ability to recognize you for what you are."

His black eyes softened and searched her face. Stella was completely at a loss for words, unable to answer him. Instead, she felt her pulse in her neck, her fingers, and, most of all, in her pussy, thudding hot and hard against her flesh.

"I swear, on my honor, I will not hurt you," he said softly. "Do you believe me?"

"Yes," Stella heard herself say. It didn't make any sense. But she did believe him. She believed him utterly.

His grip around her waist tightened and he pulled her closer. Stella felt her logic, her rationality, her willpower begin to drain away. Her body hadn't felt this way except during dreams, the kind that woke her with an orgasm and sent her searching for her vibrator. Only this was real.

The Sheikh was still smiling.

"You very nearly obeyed my command to take off your dress. You only just met me, Ms. Spencer, and you did not even know my full name, yet you very nearly undressed when I commanded you to do so. Don't you think that's unusual?"

Yes, it's unusual, Stella thought. *It's freaking insane.* She thought back to her ex, Robert: she'd never "obeyed" him in any sense of the word, though he'd never issued a command like that, either. And she wouldn't have obeyed him even if he had, just on principle. The idea of Robert ordering her to do anything was laughable.

"I really have no idea," she managed to say.

"Now you're lying," the Sheikh said, flashing his bright, white teeth. "I will be lenient now, but if you lie to me in the future..."

He pressed his thumb into her cheek, let his hand fall down the skin of her neck, smoothed his fingers over her bare shoulder, before grabbing the back of her head with sudden force. His lips curled in a sensual smile.

"You will be punished."

Stella shivered. How could that sound like something she wanted? But her body didn't lie.

"Listen," she stammered. "I don't know what kind of person you think I am—"

He let her go, almost propelling her away from him, and turned toward the bar. Stella loathed to admit that she immediately missed the feel of him, but she did. And she hated that she waited breathlessly for him to speak, but she did that too.

When he finally spoke, he did so with

exaggerated patience.

He said, "You signed a contract. I think that you did this because you wanted to, even if you are unable to admit that to yourself. And I think that you are standing here because you are tired of being afraid of the things that you want."

He turned around, easily stirring the ice in a cool looking drink, and looked at her with an expression of almost bored confidence. She was too stunned to respond. She wasn't used to sexy, dominant Sheikhs showing up out of nowhere and reading her mind.

"It's not really all that unusual to be afraid of what you want, Ms. Spencer," he went on. "But it is, perhaps, unusual to have the courage to face that fear."

He leaned back against the bar, and looked her up and down. The heat on her body tracked the path of his eyes, as though he were actually touching her. *I might as well be naked*, she thought wildly. *I might as well...*

"And now, the time for introductions is over," he said, and the smile faded from his face. His eyes flashed, and a muscle in his jaw twitched once, twice.

"Take off your dress," he commanded.

Startled, as if waking from a nap, Stella felt her fingers fumble with the straps, felt her hips wriggle, felt her dress fall, and looked down to find that she'd obeyed an order.

CHAPTER 3

Bashir watched Stella's face carefully. His voice seemed to sweep through her mind, clearing all doubt. She snapped to attention, as though in a hypnotic state, and shimmied out of that ill-fitting dress before she'd even realized what she was doing.

This clarity of purpose didn't last, as Bashir knew it wouldn't. She was a submissive, but that didn't mean she had fully accepted it yet. Already, new doubts and recrimination were beginning to play across the shadows of her face. It made her that much more vulnerable.

That vulnerability... He wanted to protect her. And he wanted to fuck her until she forgot her own name. *God, what is it with this woman?*

Bashir leaned forward, fighting the urge to leap to his feet and take her, to feel her soft flesh yield under his hands, to feel her lips around his already-hard cock. Her skin was alabaster white and flawless, set off by a plain black bra and matching underwear. She had obviously never expected anyone else to see such unremarkable underwear. Well, no matter. Bashir had little use for them.

"Remove your undergarments," he said.

Stella's eyes went wide, and her head began to shake before she'd even opened her mouth. He could see it was instinctual, reflexive. She probably didn't think of it as disobedience.

He would have to educate her.

"You did read the contract you just signed, didn't you, Ms. Spencer?"

Slowly, she nodded.

"What did it say?"

He saw that she was trembling a little, but she did not allow her voice to shake. "It says..." She swallowed. "It says that you would pay me, for..."

Bashir winced to hear her speak of the money first. That was not what he wanted to think about with her, with this woman who so mysteriously called to him. He pushed those thoughts out of his mind and rose, towering over her, and looked fiercely down at her. It was time to establish the rules.

"It says that I own you, Ms. Spencer."

He stepped forward quickly, before she had a chance to object, and put the flat of his hand on her soft, taut stomach. Her eyelids fluttered, but she looked rigidly ahead. She was hot to the touch.

"It says that you are *mine*, to do with as I please."

Her stomach moved under his hand in tiny little contractions, and he had to pause, momentarily overcome by the thought of how she might contract around his cock. He took a breath.

"It says that I have the right to discipline my possession if she is disobedient."

He let his hand drift lower, sliding down her quivering belly, until he felt the elastic waistband of her panties. He slipped two fingers under it, and her breath hitched.

"You have your safeword, but you do not want to use it, do you?" he said. "Remove your undergarments, Stella."

Bashir could feel the heat pouring off of her, could see her nipples beginning to harden under her thin cotton bra, would swear that he could smell her desire. She was a submissive, even if she didn't know it yet. She was a submissive for him.

With aching slowness, she reached behind her back and unclasped her bra. She let it hang from her body for a moment, and then, all in one motion, shrugged it off and let it drop to the floor.

She was his. He hadn't realized until this moment that he'd had any doubts. His relief was immense, was all out of proportion — he'd only just met her, after all. But she would truly submit, he knew that now. His erection grew to the point of pain as he looked at her naked breasts.

Her nipples were a dark pink, the same color as her lips; two pebbled and pointed reminders of her arousal. Her wide blue eyes were still closed as she worked her thumbs under the elastic of her panties and pushed them down over her hips. She kept her eyes closed as the last of her clothing piled around her feet, leaving her fully exposed.

Bashir sucked in his breath. She was beautiful. Every soft inch of her, every luscious curve, every smooth bit of skin — he wanted all of her. Her large breasts were very real, unlike the artificially inflated chests of so many of the women who threw themselves at him, and very inviting. Her vulva, with only a light dusting of fine hair, was invitingly plump. He wanted to taste her.

He wanted to make her scream.

"Very good," he said, moving slightly behind her.

He couldn't resist the temptation to dip down and kiss her neck, just below her ear. She arched toward him involuntarily, like a flower seeking the sun.

Ah, he thought. *That is one spot she likes.*

"And now we can proceed with the

evaluation," he murmured.

Immediately, she stiffened. "Evaluation?" she said.

Bashir did not answer her. She would learn that he would not repeat himself, that her role was not to question him. But he kept his hand flat on her belly, a calming presence and continual connection between them. So she was insecure. That was perhaps not entirely surprising. But despite that insecurity, she was brave enough to come this far. He liked that.

He moved in front of her, sliding his hand up her abdomen, and hefted one generous breast, his thumb toying with her nipple. "And how sensitive are these?"

She breathed deeply, and he laughed.

"Open your eyes, Stella."

The barest beat of hesitation, and she did. She turned her head, and looked directly into his eyes.

Bashir was momentarily stunned. There was no logic to his attraction to her, to what he felt when she looked at him. He was compelled to figure it out, to control it, as he did with all things. He'd solved every puzzle that had ever stymied him; he would not be defeated by this woman. He could get lost in those blue eyes. Why?

"Have you loved many men?" he asked her.

Her face hardened, but she found her voice. "What kind of question is that?"

He pinched her nipple, hard, and a little gasp of air escaped her lips.

"You will address me as Sheikh," he said. "And you will answer my questions. Do you understand?"

Another beat. He squeezed her whole breast, and watched her lower lip tremble. She was not like a polished piece of glass, like a metal instrument perfectly designed for his use, like so many of the women he met seemed to be. Stella was real. Fleshy. Human.

"Yes, Sheikh," she said, and it seemed to surprise her. Watching her come to terms, slowly, with what she really wanted would be priceless.

"Have you ever been in love?"

This time she looked away, and he could see she was fighting back the urge to cry. That was not the emotional response he had desired. Determined to make her feel something else, he dropped his hand and slipped it suddenly between her legs, and grabbed her pussy.

She gasped, her big eyes snapping back to his face. She gripped his shoulder, and leaned into him on the tips of her toes while he held her firmly between her legs.

"So let us start with an easier question," he said. "Have you ever been properly fucked?"

She opened her plump lips, closed them again. "I don't...I don't know," she finally said. "No."

Her breath was ragged, dragging over her words in an odd rhythm, and her stomach fluttered. He smiled.

"And you are not of the Volare."

"No," she rasped.

"But you know of us. You know what it means to be Volare."

"Yes." Her eyes were half-closed now as warmth spilled out of her and into his hand.

"And yet you have never wished to participate?"

"It wasn't..." She was struggling. "It wasn't my thing. Oh God!" she said as he dipped his middle finger into her, sliding in easily through her wet folds, and forcing himself deep inside her. She was obviously already excited.

"Until now," he said, and she groaned.

Bashir wanted to groan, too, wanted to let slip his own lust and have her right there, right then, but something stopped him. She was unlike any woman he had ever encountered, and he couldn't bring himself to squander an opportunity for something greater, even if he didn't fully understand it.

She moaned into his shoulder again, and he felt her lips part against his arm. His erection throbbed angrily for release. That flash of sincerity, of openness, when he'd asked about love, had aroused him like nothing in his memory. *Is this what it's like for normal people?*

Are they accustomed to such intimacy?

It had both invigorated and weakened him, like a drug. And, like a drug, he needed more. From her. And yet she was plainly guarding some great wound. She'd shut down just as quickly as she'd opened up. Already it was maddening. And already, Bashir knew he needed to help her, just as much as he needed to have her.

"I have rules," he said into her hair, and his voice, even to him, sounded strained. He moved his finger inside of her, just to hear her whimper, and she fell into him a little more.

"One: you will have no more need for undergarments," he said, beginning to slowly fuck her with his finger, "because you will always, *always* be accessible to me. Do you understand?"

Her fingers dug into his arm. "Yes," she said.

"Two: you will obey me, in all things, without question. Disobedience will be punished."

She nodded as her hips began to move against him. He reached up with his free hand and grabbed a mass of brown hair and pulled her head back, forcing her to look at him.

"Three: you will not come, Stella, unless I command it, and you will come exactly when I command it. I will train you to do these things. And I will tell you this: I will not take you until you beg me for it. Until you submit to my satisfaction, and you beg. And you will beg. I promise you, Stella, you will beg."

She looked at him with those open, unbelieving eyes. Bashir watched a wave of gooseflesh spread across her naked body, and took his hand away from her. She moaned again, this time almost painfully, and he tightened his grip on her hair.

It was so very difficult not to spread her before him and plunge deeply, blindly into her. But he wanted more from her. For some damnable reason, he needed more.

"Do you understand?" he said.

"Yes," she said, and her eyes flashed with frustration even as her chest still heaved. "Yes, I understand, you —"

"Careful," Bashir murmured. "I haven't decided how best to discipline you yet, Stella, but that certainly won't stop me."

He thought she might actually provoke him, she looked so excited. Not of the Volare! She was already playing the submissive's game.

She licked her lips and took a calming breath. "You haven't decided yet?"

He let her go, denying her further contact with him, lest she think she'd gained the upper hand. Ignoring her question, Bashir gestured at her dress, lying rumpled on the floor, as he moved back to the minibar.

"You may put your dress—and only your

dress — back on," he said. "Unless you prefer to continue to the Black Room in the nude? I'm feeling indulgent."

"In the nude?"

He resisted the urge to smile at her shock. So public nudity garnered a visceral reaction. Another clue to what made Stella Spencer tick. Perhaps another clue to whatever wound she was hiding. Whatever it was, Bashir would make her reveal it. He would show her her true nature before the weekend was over. And he'd make her come, screaming his name.

"Sheikh?" she said, testing out the title as she pulled her dress up. She hesitated, and then looked at him. "Why are we going to the Black Room?"

Now Bashir flashed his biggest smile. "You didn't think your evaluation was over, did you?"

CHAPTER 4

Stella's mind was not a quiet place as she followed Sheikh Bashir through the dim corridors of Club Volare. It was like a radio tuned between stations, in the middle of nowhere between towers: a gibbering crowd of warring voices, none of them making any damn sense at all.

She guessed this must be halfway normal reaction to a very abnormal experience. As ridiculous as it might sound, it had felt—*did* feel, even now, only a few moments later—as though Sheikh Bashir honest-to-God had her under some kind of spell. Stella had been in some other space, some other plane of reality, just long enough to take her clothes off and let him touch her. The intensity of that had been unlike anything else she'd ever experienced. And now it was like he'd released her just a little bit, let just a little slack in the line, to give her a chance to catch her breath.

And now, trotting dumbly behind him, her mind was running out that slack at about a hundred miles per hour.

First of all, a *Sheikh?* Really? She wasn't over that, not by a long shot. Stella had a whole bunch of questions, obviously, mostly having to do with her own immediate assumptions, which she was pretty sure were shamefully ignorant, but kind of bugged her at the back of her mind anyway. For example: harems. She cringed at the word, but couldn't help but wonder if they really existed. Or if Sheikh Bashir had one. She didn't love the idea of that.

But of course all of that paled in comparison to whatever had just come over her in that room.

If you'd asked Stella Spencer, not twenty minutes ago, if she would ever agree to essentially sell herself to a strange man, to a Dominant, a Sheikh from some foreign country she'd never heard of, for any amount of money, and then would just...*obey* when he ordered her to take her clothes off...that she'd just allow him to put his fingers inside her, that she'd accept the idea of *discipline*...

Well, not in a million years.

Except, obviously, it had happened.

She had never been more turned on. She'd never felt so desirable. This gorgeous, rich, obviously intelligent man had demanded that he pay an exorbitant amount of money for her. He *wanted* her. That in and of itself was just mind-blowing, but what really got to her was how she'd reacted when he'd told her his rules.

She was not to come, except at his command. She was his. He said he would train her.

And what Stella had felt was relief. Not fear, not anger, and she hadn't even taken offense. It was a sudden relief that let her know that she hadn't even been aware of how scared she was, of how anxious she felt all the time. The idea of ceding responsibility for her pleasure was somehow... Even now, it made her hot. Stella wasn't sure how she felt about that fact, but she couldn't deny it was true, and so she'd taken the leap.

Now she was maybe regretting it. The Black Room was one of the BDSM rooms. One of the first things Lola had explained to her was that Club Volare NY was the New York presence of the Qui Volare Society, a secretive, international group committed to pursuing excellence, and even enlightenment, through sexual exploration. It had seemed a little silly, but Stella quite liked what it stood for. Qui Volare: those who fly. And it wasn't just about BDSM, though that figured into it prominently.

Like in the Black Room.

Stella hadn't spent too much time in the

Black Room. Typically, they wanted people there who were really into the lifestyle, not outsiders, even if they were club employees. And now she was tagging along on the heels of this towering Arab Adonis—*Sheikh* Arab Adonis, she reminded herself—to the Black Room, where she was to be evaluated.

Just the word made her cringe. *Evaluation.* What did that even mean? For some reason the first memory that forced its way into her scattered brain was of a horrible gym class in third grade, when they'd been graded on their ability to do various exercises. The winners had gotten Presidential merit badges, while the losers just got to feel crappy about themselves.

And what if she failed? If it was an evaluation, there must be some way to fail. What if she wasn't good enough for this, either? The old fear and anxiety were crawling back up her spine, looking for a way to take root in her mind. Stella didn't think she could take another rejection. She'd only just begun to get through most days without crying about the last time she'd been rejected.

Don't think about that, she thought, and clamped down. *Shut it down, Stella.*

She wouldn't have the luxury of any more angst. They'd arrived.

Sheikh Bashir put one massive hand on an onyx door handle, which was set in a large, carved door of painted black wood, and turned to look her up and down. His lips curled in an appreciative smile.

"Uncross your arms, Stella," he said. "Do not hide your breasts. They are beautiful."

She hadn't even realized that she'd crossed them. He was right. She felt exposed without a bra, but she obeyed. The idea of going into the Black Room like that—loose and vulnerable— plucked at all her insecurities. Her anxiety and discomfort were just about to overtake the relief he'd given her in his room, when he wrapped his free arm around her waist and pulled her to him in a crushing kiss.

His lips were soft, but his kiss was demanding. He forced her lips apart and probed her tongue with his own with a steady, insistent pressure. And the longer it went on, the more the heat between them grew into a burning, pulsing point, until it was strong enough to melt away all of Stella's anxieties.

Too quickly, Sheikh Bashir pulled away, leaving Stella slightly stunned, and before she could ask what had just happened, he'd opened the door.

"After you, Stella," Sheikh Bashir said, his dark eyes glittering.

Stella looked ahead. There was nothing but darkness and the unknown. She had the feeling she'd never be quite sure of what might happen next around Sheikh Bashir. But then she thought about that kiss.

And once more, she made the leap.

CHAPTER 5

Stella heard the sounds first.

The entrance to the Black Room was cloaked, in a way — there was a sort of foyer, draped in black velvet, which opened to a narrow hall that twisted and turned, so that by the time you emerged into the Black Room proper, you weren't quite sure where you were in relation to the exit. And so that you couldn't see what was going on before you got there.

So she heard the sounds first. Like hard leather smacking against soft skin, in a regular rhythm, always followed by a little groan. Someone was being flogged, and someone was enjoying it.

Stella tried to hide her discomfort. She knew it was consensual, but she didn't think she'd ever quite understand the idea of pain as pleasure. Intellectually, it made sense that it could provide some relief through catharsis, but...well, maybe it wasn't supposed to be an intellectual pursuit.

"Hmmm," the Sheikh murmured, and Stella looked up to find he was watching her.

That's right, she thought. *This is an evaluation.*

As if she needed to be more nervous.

They turned the final corner of the narrow entrance hall, and there it was at the far end of the low-ceilinged room: a huge St. Andrew's Cross, with a woman tied to it, red marks all over her body. There was a man in black leather holding a flogger, and whispering in her ear intently.

The Sheikh said, "Does this bother you?"

Stella felt his intense gaze upon her once again. Somehow it seemed incredibly foolish to lie.

"I don't know," she said. "Maybe. I don't know a lot of things, I guess. I told you this isn't really my thing."

The Sheikh raised an eyebrow, but said nothing. *Great*, Stella thought. *Did I blow it already? And why do I care if I did?*

She was almost entirely wrapped up in her own thoughts again by the time the Sheikh had led her to a small booth in the back. The room was arranged for a broad range of tastes, with several tables, booths, and couches set up along the walls, and various play areas in the middle. Besides the St. Andrew's Cross, there were other specialized pieces of furniture, most of which Stella wasn't familiar with, and a few stage areas.

The Sheikh said, "But do you see anything that interests you, Stella?"

Stella was too curious to be irritated at the amusement in his voice. She found herself imagining all sorts of the things, things she normally wouldn't have the temerity to even fantasize about — they were just too ludicrous. That bench, over there, for example...

"What is *that*?" Stella said, pointing in disbelief. It was a sort of table, with stirrups — *those* could only be for one thing — and there were various restraints and chains and pulleys and all sorts of incredibly complicated looking equipment. It looked positively medieval.

"I don't know if it has a formal name," Sheikh Bashir said, leaning back in his corner of the booth, "but I always think of it as a demonstration area."

"What's it for?"

Sheikh Bashir laughed outright, and Stella felt herself instantly redden.

"Perhaps you'll find out."

That did not help her anxiety. Her cheeks burning, Stella cast about desperately for something, anything, to occupy her attention. The rest of the equipment was not something she was eager to discuss, and she'd been avoiding looking at the few other occupants of the room. In frustration, she looked directly at the smiling Sheikh.

"What about you?" she asked.

"What about me, Stella?"

"Are you married?"

Wow, where did that come from? Stella wondered. And yet, as soon as she said it, she realized it mattered. To her, anyway. She couldn't abide the idea that somewhere he had a wife, wondering where he was, or maybe doing her best *not* to wonder where he was, and she wanted to smack herself for not asking about it before. She could never be part of something like that, no matter how much money or sex or personal validation was involved.

The Sheikh leaned forward, looking at her with that spotlight intensity again. Why did it always seem like he could see right through her? How was that fair? And why was she thinking about his hands, and where he might decide to put them?

"That is important to you, isn't it?" he said.

Damn it, Stella thought. *Be wrong once, you arrogant bastard. Just once.*

But she said, "Yes." And held her head a little higher.

"Do you mean do I have many wives?" he asked. His face was unreadable, but Stella knew what he meant.

"Or a harem? Pleasure tents, perhaps? Any

kidnapping tendencies I should know about?" she said, surprised to find how much this annoyed her. Maybe because she'd been wondering the same thing only a few moments before. "I'm not totally ignorant, you know. It was a reasonable question."

Sheikh Bashir frowned. "We stopped kidnapping in the mid-nineties."

He let her stew for a moment before letting a sly smile break out across his face. She couldn't help but laugh.

"You promise?"

"Do I promise not to kidnap you and steal you away to my pleasure tent?"

"Or any other kind of tent."

He reached out and traced the line of her collarbone with one finger. Stella stopped breathing. "I don't think I could possibly make such a promise, Stella. You are too tempting. I will try my best, however."

His eyes burned like two dark coals. What could he be thinking about? What plans had he already made for her? *Stay focused, Stella.*

She took a deep breath. "Just the one wife would be enough, you know."

Sheikh Bashir smiled slightly, and brushed his fingertips against her lips. Even that touch, so delicate…she shuddered.

"No, Stella Spencer, I do not approve of infidelity," he said. "Promises are made to be kept."

It was the perfect answer, so why did Stella [suddenly] feel like crap? It probably had to do with the way the Sheikh seemed, for just a moment, to withdraw, how his forehead crinkled just a bit, how the corners of that beautiful mouth turned slightly down. Again, Stella hadn't realized how powerful it felt to be the center of his attention until all of a sudden she wasn't. She'd already begun to think of him as impenetrable and mysterious. But maybe even Sheikhs could be hurt.

"Stella," he said sharply, and Stella realized she'd become lost in her own thoughts again. She sat up straighter. Obedience to his voice was starting to seem less strange, which in and of itself was a little strange.

"Stella, we are here for a reason. Unfortunately, most club members are away for Labor Day weekend, and there are not many scenes for you to observe. You have been averting your eyes, perhaps out of a mistaken sense of propriety, but I still require you to observe what is available to us."

His voice was stern, and his expression severe. Stella hadn't felt so stung by a reprimand since grade school. The change in tone was so sudden and complete, she felt like she had whiplash. It demanded her complete attention. Alert, but slightly confused, she nodded.

"Then look, Stella. Look."

And the Sheikh pulled her roughly into the crook of his arm, against the warm heat of his hard body and the silky feel of his expensive suit, pinning her helplessly. He gently took her chin in his other hand, and turned her head towards the one place she'd been avoiding: the other occupied booth, on the other side of the room.

It looked like a group of normal businessmen enjoying an expensive dinner, except that they were being waited on by several women in what Stella thought of as the slutty Halloween version of a cocktail waitress uniform. Except with even less clothing.

She winced. She couldn't help but think about the things she'd tried to do for Robert, to help reignite the spark, or whatever the magazines were calling it now. Stella actually *had* rented a sexy maid outfit from a Halloween store. She actually *had* pranced around, waiting for him to get home. And then, when he finally had, hours later, without calling, he'd just been annoyed that now he was expected to do something else.

The humiliation had been excruciating. Somehow Stella had been supremely rejectable, even in a French maid's outfit and fuck-me heels.

But now, watching these women serve drinks in their tight tank tops with the nipples cut out, and their short skirts and garters, Stella thought back on how sexy she'd found the idea of serving her man. Maybe not necessarily Robert, specifically, not in retrospect, but...her man. That's why she'd rented the maid's outfit, and not the nurse's. She was getting a little excited just watching the scene over there.

"Ah," the Sheikh said.

You have got to be kidding me, Stella thought, reddening. *Does he really, legitimately read minds?* She squirmed a little against his grip, but that did not help. It only made her think about his touch, and how, only minutes ago, he'd nearly made her come with just his fingers and a slight pull on her hair.

And then told her he wouldn't let her come until he commanded it.

Stella's skin went hot. Why did the idea of that drive her wild?

"Stella, do not retreat into your thoughts," the Sheikh said into her ear, squeezing her to him with a delightful pressure. "I don't think you have looked hard enough. Look at the table, Stella."

One of the servant girls stepped aside, and Stella looked.

Oh. My. God.

The table wasn't a table. It was a naked woman, lying on top of a table, covered in sushi. The businessmen ate off of her as though she weren't even a person, as though her body were just part of the meal. Whoever she was, she was naked, in public, on display, like an object, a possession.

Like I'm his possession, Stella thought, and immediately her pussy began to pulse, angry for attention.

"It's called *nyotaimori*," the Sheikh said. Stella could feel his warm breath, so close to her face, and his hands on her chin, still gentle. She wished he'd let his hands roam a little further, and was instantly ashamed of herself.

"I see that you have a reaction to this, Stella," the Sheikh said. "What is it that excites you?"

"I don't know if I'm excited," Stella lied. "She's just...in *public*..."

Stella could swear she felt him smile. Something in his body changed. She was suddenly even more aware of it, next to hers, as though it exerted a real, physical force on her. *Sheikh Bashir*, she thought, *physical miracle*.

"What do you find amusing, Stella?"

"Nothing."

"Get up out of the booth," he said, and suddenly he was using that tone. That tone that brooked no disobedience. Stella froze for a moment while her brain realigned and reminded her of what she had agreed to. Slowly, she scooted her way out of the booth, sad to be leaving the warmth of Sheikh Bashir's body behind. She stood and turned to face him, inexplicably contrite. *I haven't even done anything wrong*, she thought. *What the hell is happening to me?*

The sight of Sheikh Bashir stilled all her thoughts. Somehow, he was imposing even while seated.

And those *eyes*.

"Strip," he said.

What?

Stella shook her head, glancing at the other occupants of the Black Room. They'd notice if she just took her clothes off. This wasn't like before, in the privacy of a room. Surely he didn't mean...

His face said that he did.

"As I guessed, Stella, you have both an attraction and repulsion to revealing yourself in public. Believe me when I say that we will address this in the future. But for right now," he said as he slipped out of the booth and stood far above her, "you have disobeyed a direct order, as I thought you would. And so it is time to see how you react to discipline."

CHAPTER 6

Stella gulped. *Discipline.* That word again. She had kind of just dismissed it as a joke, but the Sheikh didn't appear to be joking at all.

"Listen," she said. "I don't know if this is really…"

"You signed the contract," he said. Without even looking at her, he grabbed her wrist and began walking towards the various pieces of equipment at their end of the room.

"I'm an adult!" she said, and tried to twist from his grip.

The Sheikh turned. He didn't look angry. He didn't look upset. He only looked…completely certain.

He said, "You are an adult who signed a contract."

And he pulled her to him, twisting her arm behind her back and rendering her immobile.

Then he fixed her with that stare again, and Stella couldn't look away. It would have felt as though she were admitting her own inconstancy, her own inability to control herself, to even know herself. Somehow that was worse than whatever he had planned. And somehow, that look, those eyes, told her that he knew it, too.

And the plain fact was, she had her safeword. So why didn't she want to use it?

"Do I have to throw you over my shoulder like a petulant child, Stella?" he asked.

She grit her teeth. "No, Sheikh," she said. "I signed a contract."

Stella closed her eyes. It was almost worse, in a way, than if he'd dragged her, kicking and screaming. He hadn't had to. He'd simply pointed out that he already had a deeper control over her.

"Open your eyes, Stella."

She did. In front of her was a two tiered padded bench of sorts. To her left was a table, laid out with various instruments. A flogger. A cane. Something else that looked horrendous. She blanched.

"No," she said, shaking her head. Even the idea…

Sheikh Bashir gripped her chin again, and examined her face.

"Tell me what it is that you think you object to," he said.

"Pain," she blurted out. "I don't...you shouldn't inflict *pain* on other human beings. It's not right. There's already so much pain in the world..."

Stella's eyes began to swell with tears, and she pressed her lips together, determined not to cry. *I must look like a two year old*, she thought, and it was infuriating. Why cry? Why would this make her cry? What right did she have to be disappointed in someone she'd known for less than a day?

"Look at me, Stella," he commanded. She forced herself to comply. Sheikh Bashir's own eyes were soft, and seemed...sad? Now what the hell was going on?

"It cannot surprise you to learn that some people derive pleasure from certain kinds of controlled pain," he said.

"I know," Stella said, sniffling. "I don't understand it, but I know."

"But you are not one of them," he added.

"No."

"There are many iterations of the dynamic between Dominant and submissive, Stella. Some Dominants adhere to a form of discipline that involves genuine unpleasantness for their submissives. I take the view that if such measures are necessary, the relationship is already a failure. To me, discipline is another way to teach, and to learn. And to grow closer."

He let those words hang in the air between them. Stella couldn't be sure if they were meant for her, or if he spoke to some woman from his past. *We're all haunted by the ghosts of past relationships, aren't we?*

And then: *Wait, grow closer? With me?*

Sheikh Bashir stroked her cheek, his eyes softening. "I would never hurt you, Stella, or any other woman who did not want to be hurt. It is important to me that you know that."

"Ok," Stella managed. "Thank you."

"Good," he said, and stepped back. "Now bend over the bench."

Stella actually imagined a record scratching. What had they just been talking about? She tried to step back, but Sheikh Bashir caught her wrist.

"You must decide if you trust me, Stella Spencer. As my submissive, you will bend over this bench, and you will be disciplined. Otherwise you will leave, and our contract will be terminated."

Stella felt totally unmoored, untethered, battered about. It was ludicrous. All of this was just absurd. She had no frame of reference for situations like this, no idea what the rules were for these kinds of relationships. She looked at Sheikh Bashir's patient and immovable face, and it looked like it contained the whole world. She realized: *I don't have any idea what to do all the time anyway.* She hadn't felt like she could rely on her perceptions of people or relationships since Robert had shown her how wrong she could be about both. It was like the Sheikh only pointed out to her what her life was already like, as though, so far, every interaction with him was simply life with the volume turned way up, and with all the boring bits taken out.

Had she felt able to trust any one else since the divorce? Had she even considered the possibility? Of course she hadn't. And that seemed a terrible way to go through life.

Slowly, Stella nodded. Her feet seemed to move forward of their own accord. Her arms gripped the edge of the upper tier of the bench, and she carefully placed each knee, one and then the other, on the lower tier.

And then she bent over, resting her stomach on the upper tier, her breasts pushed forward and her eyes facing forward. She had a perfect view of the rest of the room. She would know if anyone looked back and saw her.

"Good girl," she heard the Sheikh say.

He placed his hand on the back of her neck, slipping it under her hair, and that touch made all the difference. Stella focused on the feel of his warm, rough hand as he slid it down her back, over her hip, and onto her ass, and on the fire that he left in his wake. She'd never been this responsive with anyone.

"Stella, I have made a few observations," the

Sheikh said, his unmoving hand still drawing all her attention. "You have an unquiet mind in times of stress. You are insecure. You are so preoccupied with these insecurities that I suspect it is difficult for you to feel 'in the moment.' And that," he continued, "is unfortunate."

Now the hand moved down the sensitive underside of her thigh until it reached the hem of her tight dress.

"Because I demand your full attention, Stella," he said, and began to pull her dress up.

She may have squeaked. Her naked ass was exposed to the air now, and her pussy, too. Stella gripped the end of the bench as if her life depended on it, and prayed the men on the other side of the room wouldn't look up.

Is this really happening? she thought. *Is he really going to —*

He spanked her. Hard.

The blow echoed up and down her body, obliterating all thought, all feeling, all sensation apart from where his hand connected with her ass. That it had really happened was stunning, a sideways shove that pushed her completely out of the realm of the ordinary world and forced her to take every new stimulation on its own terms.

And then he did it again. She felt his open palm cup her ass, heard the smack of flesh against flesh. Briefly she wondered whether any of the businessmen, busy with their debauched meal, might hear, might care to look up, but before her mind could follow that thought down a trail of what-ifs and worry, he spanked her again.

"What did you do wrong, Stella?" he asked, and smacked her on the other cheek.

"I…"

"I asked you a direct question." His hand connected again, this time lower, where her cheeks joined. The vibrations went straight through her pussy, and she felt her thighs shake.

"I disobeyed an order," Stella gasped.

He hit her again. She was beginning to feel light all over, as though teased with thousands of feathers, and she was having trouble focusing on anything other than the pulsing ache that gathered around her pussy.

"Will you repeat that mistake?"

She shook her head. It was not enough. "Perhaps I need to call those gentleman in the booth to act as witnesses," he said. "Perhaps I should invite them to take a turn?"

She startled, and reflexively tried to push herself off the bench, but he pushed her back down and held her there. She whimpered, and one large hand took hold of her shoulder while the other delivering a loud smack against her ass before burying two fingers in her pussy.

"No, Stella," he whispered in her ear. "That

is my prerogative, if I wish." His fingers swirled slowly inside her, building up that pressure. She wanted to come so badly, and yet, if she did, she'd have disobeyed another order, and who knew what he would do then.

"Please," she panted.

"I think you care entirely too much about what other people think, Stella," the Sheikh said. "But that is something I can use. And I will. But not yet."

And suddenly, he was gone. Stella looked wildly over her shoulder; he was already walking toward what she guessed was the entrance, with the unstated implication that she was to follow him. The sudden shift left no room for thought. Hastily she pushed her dress down and trotted after him, trying to maintain some semblance of dignity while her body still burned and her ass still stung.

"Sheikh," she began, and then realized she didn't even know what questions to ask. She was too disoriented. The pulsing in her core hadn't yet dissipated, and thinking about anything else was like trying to talk over a fire alarm. Every thought led back to how she might get him to let her come.

He grabbed her hand, and gave it a squeeze. In the dim light she could see that he was smiling.

"I know what I need to know for now, Stella Spencer," he said, still striding ahead of her.

He led her directly to the elevator bank, and pressed the button.

What? What does he know? What could he possibly have discovered?

"Now where are we going?" she asked. She pawed at the hem of her dress with her free hand, just to give herself something to do. The Sheikh's shoulders, barely contained in that fine suit, were incredibly distracting.

Sheikh Bashir did not deign to answer her, but instead simply pulled her in after him as the elevator doors opened. Stella stumbled, crashing into his chest.

That didn't help.

She stayed there, breathing in his exotic cologne and his own spicy scent, feeling the heat of his chest on her cheek. Maybe if she asked very nicely, he might let her come…

"Stella," he said.

"Mmm?"

"The door has opened."

He peeled her off his chest, and this time put his arm around her waist to guide her out of the elevator. They were on the floor just below Club Volare, where the luxury suites were located. As they approached one large, expensive looking door, Stella's brain finally caught up with the rest of her: this was a hotel suite. Men only brought women to hotel suites for one reason. This was it. She was about to get her wish.

Can I really do this?

It wasn't what she'd expected to think. She'd been so dazed by what had happened in the Black Room, by Sheikh Bashir's uncanny perceptions, by the completely unexpected way she'd responded to, well, spanking. By the way she simply responded to *him*. But now the reality of the situation, and all the attendant expectations, crowded in on her. She would technically be paid for sex. Put whatever sort of gloss you want on it, but that's what was about to happen.

And she hadn't been with anyone since her husband. Her *ex*-husband. Not since she'd been humiliated and left, not since she'd finally become convinced that she must just be crap in bed, not since...

Oh God, she thought, *what if I really am terrible? What if he decides I'm just not worth it?*

Stella fought the urge to run away as Sheikh Bashir punched in an access code and the door swung silently open. She stared rigidly ahead as he led her into the beautiful room, too anxious to even look at the Sheikh.

I can't do this, she thought. *I can't —*

"Stella," Sheikh Bashir said, and gently pulled her into another kiss.

It was even better than the first one. Softer and sweeter at first, as though he really was just trying to calm her, until he began to lose himself in it. Stella felt the lust in him, the hunger—hunger for *her*—and with gratitude she let go of all those terrible thoughts and replaced them with one word: *yes*.

But Sheikh Bashir pulled away. "Not yet, Stella," he said. "Remember my rules. You will submit, and you will beg."

A little electric thrill ran straight through her. She was almost prepared to beg *now*. And yet, what could further submission mean? The Sheikh only smiled, and dragged his hand up the side of her body to give her nipple a little pinch.

"'Til tomorrow, Stella," he said.

And just like that, he left her alone in the richest room she'd ever seen in her life.

Stella would have been embarrassed to admit how long she stood there in the foyer of her gorgeous suite with the empty look of a lobotomy patient. It took a while to return to normal levels of functioning, but when she finally did, she found everything had been provided for. There were clothes in the closets, food in the refrigerator, wine in the...well, it looked like a wine closet. A temperature controlled wine closet.

There were towels in the marble bath.

Stella did a full inventory, but eventually had to admit two things: no matter what she did, she wasn't going to get the Sheikh out of her mind, and her body wasn't going to stop telling her to get an orgasm any way she could, and that marble bath was just too inviting to pass up.

She had every intention of masturbating in that bath. And yet, to her frustration, and with no small amount of wonder, she found that she couldn't.

The incredible truth was that she didn't want to disobey Sheikh Bashir al Aziz bin Said. Stella Spencer wouldn't come until he commanded it.

CHAPTER 7

She was truly a rare find.

Bashir hadn't had this much fun with a woman since Cambridge, only this time, he was aware of the woman's true intentions. With no surprises waiting in the wings, he was free to simply enjoy her. And Stella Spencer was a continual source of joy. It was as though she were incapable of dishonesty or calculation, and putting a surprised smile on her face was quickly becoming Bashir's favorite pastime.

He wished he could have stayed the previous night, to see her reaction to the room and all the little comforts he'd requested, but Bashir was only human. If he'd stayed, he would have spent all night inside her, but it wouldn't have been the quite the experience he knew it could be for either of them. Some things took time and preparation.

At least now he got to see her reaction to the dress.

"Is this real?" she said, holding it up at arm's length like it was some sort of priceless artifact. She was wrapped in one of the hotel's plush cotton robes, and nothing else. Her hair was still slightly damp, and her soft, pale skin had a certain glow to it. The effect was...distracting. Bashir kept wondering what she tasted like.

Ridiculous, he thought. *Stay focused.*

"I am told it is made by a very important designer," Bashir said. "You may, of course, keep it. It has been tailored to your measurements."

Stella looked at him as though he had spoken in tongues, then burst out laughing.

"I'm sorry," she said, and blushed, which was yet another distraction for Bashir's tortured cock. "I don't mean to be rude. It's an incredible gift. I just have no idea where I could wear something like this."

"You will wear it tonight," Bashir said, "while you serve me at an event that I am obligated to attend."

Her round blue eyes widened, and her lips parted as she caught her breath. *Delightful.*

"Serve you?" she said.

"You recall the service you saw yesterday in the Black Room?" Bashir asked. She nodded, and her robe fell open an inch more as she remembered to breathe. It was too much. Bashir crossed to her and buried his hand in her robe. Her nipples were already hard.

"Yes," she said faintly. He had surprised her, but now her eyes were half-closed. Bashir rolled her breast in his hand with satisfaction. She should feel at least some of the torture that he did.

"You will serve me as they did," he said. "You will anticipate my needs, you will obey my commands, and if I so desire it, you will bend over so that I may take you in that expensive dress, wherever and whenever I feel like it. Or even if I simply want to enjoy the view. Is that clear?"

He saw the shiver run through her.

"Yes," she said.

"Good," Bashir said. "Now I want to watch you get dressed. Take off this damn robe."

~ ~ ~

Bashir found the Alexandria Club to be quite boring, but it was often where Cantabridgian events were held in New York. Foolish, really; Cambridge alumni could certainly afford their own building. But Bashir knew his irritation wasn't entirely due to the environs. He no longer had the best associations with these events. They used to be bearable only because Mark would be there, and they'd have as much fun as they'd had at

Cambridge together.

That was all in the past, of course. Mark would not be there.

But Cecil Creighton would. Bashir knew him in college mainly by reputation, as an ass, and now, later in life, as a powerful executive at the international construction firm his family still controlled. There were only so many people in the world one could turn to if one needed an oil pipeline built quickly, and there were even fewer if one needed it to go undetected so that one might siphon off the oil reserves of one's neighbor. Creighton was one of those men, and Bashir strongly suspected that he had been in contact with groups who wished to steal from Ras al Manas. Protecting the assets of his country — and his family — was a responsibility he could not shirk, even if he would much rather have stayed in the confines of Volare with Stella.

Stella. She stood next to him on the landing above the main hall, bursting from the low scoop neck of her tight, expensive black dress, failing entirely to hide her nervousness. Again, it charmed him. Even with the pain she worked so hard to hide, with what he'd come to think of as the great wound, even with that wearing her down, she still managed to be open to the world. She was like a raw nerve that wouldn't flinch. The combination of bravery and vulnerability was both inspiring and...

Bashir stopped himself short. That was not a productive avenue of thought. Undoubtedly Stella Spencer unnerved him, undoubtedly she was special, but it was unlikely she would be a miracle match for him. Or, even if she was, that she'd be ready for it, or that he could trust her to remain true. He wouldn't get his hopes up, not when the likely outcome was an inevitable political marriage.

An inevitability that would certainly come sooner rather than later, if he could not convince Creighton that it was in his interest to ally with Ras al Manas. His family's patience for his proclivities was always in direct proportion to his usefulness.

"Stella," he said, frowning. She seemed distracted, peering down below at the mass of well dressed, powerful people milling about the large, well appointed hall. He needed her to remember why she was here. He needed her to be present.

"Yes, Sheikh?"

"Display your breasts for me."

She jerked her head back, and then turned toward him, obviously not certain if she had heard correctly.

"Here?" she said, and looked down again at the party below. They were alone on the landing, but, of course, anyone might look up at any time. Which was the point. Bashir glowered.

"If I have to repeat myself, Stella," he said, "you'll spend the rest of the night that way."

She looked up and blanched. She could tell he was serious.

Bashir saw her hands shake slightly as she raised them to her breasts, and knew it meant that she was experiencing a spike in adrenaline, in focus, in sensation. She hesitated, only momentarily, and when he frowned she moved quickly, as though plunging ahead, and pulled her dress down over her nipples.

"Do not close your eyes, Stella," he said, and reached out to brush her cheek. "Be aware, in this moment. Be fully in this moment, or you will have failed to serve me."

Tension colored her face at the mention of failure. Another interesting tidbit.

Obediently, she opened her eyes, her pupils full and black, pushing the blue of her irises into a fine, bright ring. So open to the world. So brave, in her way. Bashir let his hand trail lightly down her neck to tweak one sensitive nipple, and smiled when she jumped.

"Remember that I own you, Stella," he said. "Remember that you are mine, that you are here to serve me, that you will feel what I tell you to feel, when I tell you to feel it. We begin tonight."

She swayed slightly, beneath his touch, and

once again Bashir had to fight the urge to simply ravish her. "Clothe yourself," he said. "I have business to attend to. And then I will attend to you."

CHAPTER 8

Stella did *not* like Cecil Creighton. She didn't like how he kept throwing back those scotch and sodas, she didn't like the way his fleshy face ruddied the more he drank, she didn't like the way he wore his sense of entitlement like a suit of impenetrable armor, and she didn't like the way he didn't even bother to hide the way he looked her at her.

Which made it all the more confusing that she was somehow very excited to be sitting on the Sheikh's lap while the two of them talked. The Sheikh had found them a private room off the main hall, full of books and what looked like actual illuminated manuscripts hidden away under protective glass. It wasn't technically "in public," but Stella was very aware of Creighton's eyes upon her. And she was very aware that Creighton knew she belonged, in the very literal sense, to Sheikh Bashir.

She shook her head slightly, biting her lip to keep from smiling. *Belonged to Sheikh Bashir.* How easily she'd thought that. How easily it had made her wet. *This is nuts.*

But as long as Sheikh Bashir held her, it felt as thought no one else really mattered. Creighton didn't matter, except as a spectacle. It was like Sheikh Bashir had provided her with a tiny audience, just to excite her. And it did.

"Where'd you find her?" Creighton asked, pulling her out of her thoughts. His red-rimmed eyes were covetous. Again, Stella was torn between disgust and arousal. They spoke of her as if she really were just a possession.

Sheikh Bashir tightened his arm about her waist, and lifted the other hand to absently fondle her breast. *Oh my God, he's really doing that.* Stella felt her nipples harden, and knew they would be visible through her dress. "It wouldn't matter," Sheikh Bashir was saying. "She's one of a kind, and she's mine."

I'm his. Stella's insides fluttered at his words, even if she wasn't sure he meant them. She hadn't felt that rush in ages.

"But we were talking about pipelines."

Creighton rolled his eyes.

"You know, I get tired of pipelines. All day,

every day, it's pipelines. And really, it's impossible to concentrate with her in the room, Bashir. Tell me where you got her. Or at least let me borrow her."

Stella stiffened. Was that part of the arrangement? Would Sheikh Bashir do it? She'd thought he'd only been messing with her in the Black Room when he suggested something like that, but he obviously wanted something from this cretin. But he wouldn't just pass her around like a party favor, would he? Not after he'd just laid claim to her?

That was one of those things that, in theory, made Stella incredibly hot, but in practice, right now, with Cecil Creighton? No. And, in truth, she wanted Sheikh Bashir to want her for himself.

Wait, when did that happen?

"Exquisite, no?" Sheikh Bashir said, and slipped his hand under her dress, between her legs. Stella reddened; he would feel how wet she was. How she was probably already seeping through the thin dress. And, oh God, Cecil Creighton was watching all of it.

Sheikh Bashir's seductive smile demanded all of her attention. "So responsive," he said.

He forced her thighs apart and ran his fingers up and down her slit, testing her. Through half-lidded eyes she could see that he smoldered. Would he take her right there? No, he couldn't. That was insane. But she realized she still wanted him to, even with Cecil Creighton looking on. The admission sent an immediate bolt of electricity from her brain to her pussy and back again, clearing her mind as she began to grind her hips into his hand. She put her arms around his neck and sighed.

"Christ, Bashir," she heard Creighton say. It both demeaned and thrilled her.

What has he done to me? Why do I like this? The thought floated up unbidden and darted away just as quickly, a tiny insignificance in the immense ocean of sensation that flooded through her. Sheikh Bashir thrust a finger into her, and she clenched around it gladly, happy to have another feeling to wrap herself around. Her mind was almost completely empty, making room for more and more feeling. She hadn't even realized how much anxiety and sadness she'd become accustomed to carrying around with her, and now Sheikh Bashir was able to banish it with just a finger. Somehow, the fact that she was being watched, that she had an audience, only intensified everything.

Until Sheikh Bashir abruptly stopped. With a soft chuckle, he withdrew his hand entirely.

Not again, she silently railed. *When is he going to let me come?*

"Get up and serve us another round, pet," he said. "Mr. Creighton is running low again."

Creighton rattled the ice in his otherwise empty glass for emphasis, and the hollow crack of ice cubes dragged Stella back down to earth. She pretended to smooth her dress in an effort to steady herself. Every encounter with Sheikh Bashir seemed to go deeper than the one before, seemed to cast her further away from herself and closer to...what?

Pretty soon I won't be able to think at all. Stella was surprised to find that she looked forward to that moment.

"'Nother scotch. Macallan is fine. You'd think they'd have better scotch at these things," Creighton said. He didn't even remark on what had just happened, as though rich and powerful men toyed with women like that all the time. As far as Stella knew, maybe they did.

Sheikh Bashir slipped a hand under her dress as she rose, and gave her ass a sharp pinch.

"Quickly."

Her spine straightened, and her cheeks felt hot as Creighton laughed after her. It gave her the weirdest sense of *déjà vu*, and she was almost to the bar before she realized why: Robert, of course. Robert used to make her attend events that were almost like this, had dragged her along as a necessary accessory while he tried to conduct business. Only he had always been disappointed in her, and had inevitably laughed her off in the same derisive tone that Creighton had used. He'd hated how naïve she was, how, in his words, everyone could read her face like an open book. Robert would explain to her over and over again that information was the currency of the broker business, and he needed a poker player by his side, not a patsy.

There were so many parallels, and yet she'd been enjoying herself up until this moment, even with Creighton there. Why? What was so different about the Sheikh?

The Sheikh. It was still too absurd.

Stella's mind whirred back to life as she collected the drinks and began to make her way back to the little private room with the sliding paneled doors. She had enjoyed the non-thinking, physically present respite she got with the Sheikh, but it seemed important that she figure this out. Thinking about Robert had deflated her mood a little, and she was angry about that. She wanted to hold onto the high that the Sheikh gave her, even if she didn't understand it completely. Even if it was, in its way, sort of horrifyingly embarrassing. It was still the one bright spot in the past few horrible months, and she only had the weekend, after all.

What *was* it about him? She couldn't help but think about the Sheikh's promise: she would beg. She would come on his command. She would submit. What did that even mean? She felt she'd submitted pretty well so far;

wasn't that good enough? What did he want? What did she have to do to get him to...

Wow, Stella thought. *I'm seriously trying to figure out how to get him to fuck me.* It was incredible that she was thinking like this when he had promised to pay *her* for the privilege. The Sheikh really was naturally dominant, naturally powerful. She couldn't help but think about how best to serve him.

Or maybe I truly am submissive.

That thought struck her just as she slid open the door with her foot and slipped into the room, and it might have thrown her for a loop if she didn't already feel two pairs of eyes on her. She didn't want to embarrass the Sheikh, or herself. She didn't want to fail at her task, and she didn't want to reveal herself to be a confused, muddled mess inside, not to someone like Creighton, just for reasons of pride, and especially not to Sheikh Bashir, for reasons that Stella knew were best left unexamined at the moment.

Focus on the task at hand, she thought. *Focus on serving him.*

That this was part of their arrangement, for lack of a better word, that she was obeying a direct command from the Sheikh, imbued every little gesture with a significance it wouldn't normally have had. As she walked over to where the two men sat in those wide leather chairs, she let her hips swing and pushed her breasts out. She took pride in the way she bent at the waist and gracefully extended her arm, not caring that Creighton leered at her. This was for the Sheikh. This was part of the game.

And the sight of him, straight backed, hands gripping either armrest, his tailored suit jacket open and relaxed, revealing a crisp white shirt stretched taut over that broad chest...

It was enough to take any woman's breath away.

She tried not to tremble as she held his drink forward, and, as he took it, she moved her finger up the side of the glass, just to touch him again.

Wow, Stella, get a hold of yourself. This is not middle school.

But the Sheikh knew. From the curl of his lip, she could tell he knew.

"Well done," he said, and Stella smiled.

Then came Creighton's voice from behind her. "I'd love for my bitch ex-wife to see me with a piece like that, waiting on me hand and foot," he said. "Just to see her face. Didn't give her a damn thing in the divorce, either. She probably *is* waiting tables."

And he laughed.

Stella cringed; just the word 'divorce' was enough to crash through the little cocoon she'd built up around herself while serving the drinks. And the Sheikh noticed.

She stood up, more quickly than she intended to. She wouldn't let them see her falter. Wouldn't let the Sheikh see her falter. The idea that he would see her like that, broken and hurt and damaged, was just unbearable. It would ruin everything this weekend had promised to be. She didn't want to be that discarded, unlovable woman with him; she wanted to be the sexy, desirable woman who was worth a small fortune.

"Can I get you anything else, Sheikh?" she said. But she couldn't meet his eyes, even though she felt his gaze, studying her.

"Creighton?" the Sheikh finally said.

"Yeah, all right, Bashir," Creighton said, and Stella turned to find him rising unsteadily to his feet. He was drunker than she'd thought.

"Listen, Bashir, I can't just drop a contract, but let me make a phone call and see if I can't work something out," he continued. He licked his lips, and looked longingly at Stella's breasts. "Those bastards won't have the money for repeat business, anyway. Maybe I can give you a little information, just between us. What you do with it is your business. In return for a little consideration, of course."

And he gave the Sheikh one of those hard looks that Stella remembered from Robert's negotiations. He might be a drunk, but Creighton wasn't stupid. She wondered what kind of deal they'd worked out when she went to get the drinks, and then realized she didn't really care. She only cared that it meant she'd be alone with Sheikh Bashir soon.

When did I get such a one-track mind? she wondered as she watched Creighton fumble with the door. Finally he set his drink down on a side table and manhandled the thing open. He really was drunk.

Stella turned, eager to hear what the Sheikh had in store for her next, only to see him rise out of his own chair. He didn't even look at her as he buttoned his suit jacket closed.

"I'll be back shortly," he said.

"What?" Stella had never been so disappointed. "But why—"

He turned on her. "I have my own phone call to make. You will wait for me here. You will think about how to please me while you wait. And if you say another word, you will do it naked."

Whoa. No matter how adventurous she'd become, Stella did *not* want that.

"Yes, Sheikh," she said, and watched him stride out of the room.

CHAPTER 9

She was just supposed to wait? That sucked. Or rather, it didn't entirely suck; Stella found that, with even just a little bit of leeway, her imagination began to run wild. How *could* she please him? What sort of things might he order her to do next? He kept hinting at having her do...*things* in public, and the idea terrified her. But if she were being completely honest, it terrified her because it also excited her.

Or what about when he'd spanked her? That was an entirely new kind of thrill. Seriously, she'd been *spanked*. She still couldn't believe it.

But the real question, of course, was whether he'd ever actually fuck her. God, what if he didn't? What if he decided he didn't want to? She shook her head, clearing it of that unbearable thought. He would. And yet, it was another thing she awaited with both anticipation and fear. She'd been so afraid that he'd just immediately get down to it, and she'd felt like, well, a whore, but that was apparently not the Sheikh's style. By the time he got around to it, maybe she really would beg.

And, more than that even, what about his claim that he would train her? What did that even mean? She wasn't sure she believed that anyone could ever make her come on command, though the idea was...incredibly hot. The thought of being so completely in the Sheikh's power made her feel both unsteady and somehow free, as though she had gained the ability to fly, but only while drunk.

She laughed. What a weird thought. And it didn't totally do justice to the warmth pooling between her legs, or the faint tingling sensation that washed over her skin in steady waves.

He's not even in the room and I feel like this, she thought. *He's like a drug.*

And so she couldn't hold back her smile when she heard the doors slide open. Stella looked up, ready to recite a litany of ways she hoped to please the Sheikh.

Only to find Cecil Creighton standing over her.

"Forgot my drink," Creighton said.

Stella tried to keep a neutral expression. "It's over there, by the door."

"So it is."

Creighton ambled back in the direction he'd come, but when he reached the little table, he didn't retrieve his drink. He closed the door.

Stella tensed. It was a crowded party, and yet those heavy wood doors blocked out all sound. And she couldn't think of a reason for Creighton to close that door that wasn't terrible.

Just act natural, she thought. *Keep things normal.* "What are you doing?" she said.

Creighton smiled at her. "I just wanna talk," he said. "Just want to suss out prices, you know? I'm a businessman."

Stella moved behind one of the high backed leather chairs, taking hold of the top with her hands, as though she could somehow maneuver it if she had to. She just felt better with something between her and Creighton.

"Aw, c'mon," Creighton said, and walked toward her. "Don't be frightened. I just wanna know how much Bashir paid, that's all."

Stella recoiled, stepping back until she bumped up against a bookcase. There was nowhere to go, and nowhere to hide, not from Creighton, and not from what he'd just said. Sheikh Bashir *was* paying her, but it wasn't like that, not really, was it? If that's all it was, he would have just had his way with her and that would be it. There wouldn't be all this stuff about how she felt, and her fears, and...

But what could someone like Sheikh Bashir

possibly see in her? Was she just deluding herself?

She wanted to cry, she was so angry. There was no way a man like Creighton would ever understand any of that, especially not if Stella wasn't sure she did, herself.

"Go to hell," she said.

"I'll double it," Creighton said, spreading his arms wide. Like he was doing her a favor. Being reasonable.

"Seriously, go to hell," Stella said viciously. "I'm not for sale, you...unbelievable *pig*. And not even if you were the last man on earth."

Oh, that was probably not smart.

Creighton's face darkened. Stella could see the rage building in him, slowly, as all the little thoughts and insults and entitlements took more time to knot together, to grow, fighting through the haze of alcohol to join together into one massive cumulus cloud of fury.

"What did you just say?" he whispered.

But Stella didn't need to repeat it. It looked like Creighton's wounded pride was gushing anger and bile, filling him to the brim, and Stella's silence only seemed to make it worse. His face grew bright red, and his eyes bulged. He knocked over an end table that stood between them, shattering empty glasses on the floor.

Oh God, Stella thought. *He's really crazy*.

"What did you just say, you little bitch?"

Creighton hissed, and he darted forward, putting himself squarely between Stella and the door. There was a terrible, still moment when neither of them moved. And then Stella made a break for the exit, running around the other side of the chair. But even drunk, Creighton was quick, and the room was not large, and there were too many things in Stella's way.

He caught her. He grabbed her by the arm, his hot fingers digging painfully into her flesh, and he threw her back against a wall of books. Stella lost her balance and fell to her knees, crumpled in a heap of old books, too shocked to even cry out. Was this really happening? Did people really do things like this to each other?

"Now how much?" Creighton sneered, standing over her.

"Please don't hurt me," was all Stella could say.

But she was certain he would.

Or would *have*. They both turned at the sound of the sliding doors opening: Sheikh Bashir stood at the other end of the room, his eyes burning.

"Did he hurt you?" he said, very quietly.

"Not really," Stella said. "But I think he was going to." She'd be damned if she would lie for Creighton. She would knock him out herself if she could.

Like he could read her thoughts, Sheikh Bashir turned on Creighton, a nimbus of pure malevolence swirling around him. He looked positively murderous. Creighton fell back, away from Stella, as if he could somehow wash his hands of it.

"Bashir—"

"Shut up," Sheikh Bashir said, and then he pounced.

Creighton dashed behind a side table, but Sheikh Bashir simply tossed it aside. Stella covered her ears and her head against the flying books and glass and alcohol, and when she looked up, Sheikh Bashir had Creighton by the wrist and throat.

The Sheikh forced the cretin to his knees.

"You are scum, Creighton," he said. "You are entitled scum, and you are not fit to be in the same room with her. That I allowed this to happen..."

Sheikh Bashir inhaled deeply, and twisted Creighton's wrist away from his body. Creighton blubbered, unable to cry out through his strangled throat.

"Apologize, Creighton. Crawl, on your hands and knees, and apologize. And if she accepts, I'll let you leave here in one piece."

"Sheikh Bashir," Stella said.

Startled, the Sheikh relaxed his grip on Creighton's throat, and let the drunken, would-be assailant fall to the floor, choking.

The Sheikh himself lurched sideways, his face twisted with emotion as he tried to switch gears.

"Stella," he said, and stopped. It seemed the first time Stella had seen him at a loss for words. He looked at her blankly, his helplessness here in stark contrast to the way he physically dominated the room.

"I just want him to leave," she said quietly.

Slowly he nodded. "As you wish," he said, and he bent down to grab Creighton by the back of the neck. The Sheikh dragged the still-blubbering Creighton to the doors, pausing only to say something Stella couldn't quite hear. Whatever it was, Creighton nodded visibly — gratefully, even. And then he fled from the room.

Sheikh Bashir closed the doors after him. He took a deep breath, his broad shoulders rounding under his silk suit, and turned around. His handsome face was stricken.

"There is no apology I can make for having failed you so completely," he said.

What?

Stella was almost annoyed at him. Pretty much every stress hormone in her body was bouncing around chaotically inside her, and she felt like a shaken grab bag of emotion, but she was still pretty sure that none of things she was feeling was anger towards Sheikh Bashir. In fact, she was feeling pretty damn grateful to the tall, incredibly strong, gorgeous man who'd just defended her.

"You didn't do anything wrong," she said.

He shook his head. "I left you alone," he said, crossing the room in a few long strides. "I showed you off to a man I didn't know well, and then I left you alone and unprotected. It is unforgiveable."

He stood so close, and yet, he seemed lost in himself. In a kind of self-loathing. The sight of him, standing before her, opening and closing his fists, jaw clenching, full of recrimination and regret, pushed every panic button Stella had. This was what people looked like just before things got bad. Just before they wanted to leave. All she wanted to do was make it better.

She said, "Really, it's fine." But even to her, it sounded shrill, brittle, fragile. *Maybe I'm more shaken up than I thought.* But why would Sheikh Bashir want anything to do with someone who was so much trouble? Wasn't this supposed to be a fun weekend?

"Be still." He interrupted her thoughts to hold the side of her face, and took a moment to inspect her arm. He frowned, then locked his eyes with hers. "A Dominant doesn't just assume control, Stella. They assume responsibility. You are under my control, and thus your safety is my responsibility. I came very close to failing you."

His fingers brushed lightly over the red marks that Creighton had left on her skin; Stella could tell she would probably bruise. "I did fail you," he said sadly.

But his touch electrified her. Every point of contact between them provided a focus for the nervous energy that bubbled inside her, for all the fear, the adrenaline, the anger. It all rushed to the surface where he touched her, much like the blood forming a bruise under her skin, and suddenly, she wanted him. She wanted him to want her. She wanted him to know it.

"You came back," she said. "And you protected me."

Stella paused; that wasn't what she'd meant to say at all. It just came out. She had never expected anyone to do either of those things, and yet, a man she'd only just met had done them, and now she was piling on the pressure like some kind of clinger. She looked down at her feet, ashamed.

"I'm sorry," she said again, "I didn't mean —"

Sheikh Bashir's hand, moving down from her face to her breast, silenced her. He pushed his warm hand under her dress, brushing his thumb over her nipple, kneading the full, swelling flesh. Stella felt her back arch slightly as her breath hitched.

"Only apologize when you have done something wrong, Stella," he said.

Stella closed her eyes. She could feel the Sheikh's eyes on her, could tell they once more saw more than she ever wanted to reveal. She didn't want to be the bitter, wounded, broken divorcée with him; she didn't want to be the little girl everyone was always leaving. She wanted to be the glamorous, sexy, daring woman who could sell herself for a weekend and not give a damn.

The Sheikh pushed her against the bookcase, kicking the books at his feet out of the way, and pulled her breast free of her too-expensive dress. He took her wrists gently in hand, and pinned them above her head.

Then he just looked at her. It felt like her whole body seemed to shake and shiver, pulled taut for him, like a string he could pluck at his leisure.

"Stella," he said, and his voice had gone deep, guttural. He ran his hand down the length of her body, up and down, returning to her aching breast, and claimed her mouth with his.

Stella arched into him, needing to feel his body against hers in as many places as possible. She'd never wanted anyone so badly, never felt the need for completion more in her entire life. There were too many things built up inside her, and they needed release.

"Please," she said.

He kissed her neck, and she felt it in her clit.

She felt everything in her clit.

"Tell me why you would apologize for that, Stella," he murmured into her skin.

God no, she thought. *Don't make me be that person. Just…please…let me be…*

"Please," she said, feeling completely helpless. "Please just take me back to the hotel. You can do anything you want."

I can't believe I just said that, she thought. *Have I begged? Is that good enough?*

He laughed, and hefted her leg up around his waist, running his hand up the underside of her thigh.

"No, Stella," he said, tightening his grip on her wrists. "I do not need your permission, remember? I will do anything that I want. I will do *everything* that I want. But first, I want you to answer my questions."

Stella shook her head, and then moaned as he rolled his hips against her swollen clit.

"Please…" And she had to stop herself, because suddenly, insanely, she felt like she might cry from the frustration, and the stress, and everything that had happened to her in the last six months. Actually cry, in front of him. And that was unacceptable.

"Stella," he said. "Look at me."

She breathed deep, and obeyed. He looked into her, and she felt naked. All of the things she struggled to hide—her anxiety, her nervousness, her desperation to hide every bad thing she felt—all of them betrayed her, rose to the surface, showed themselves in her face. She turned away, trembling with tension.

"You need to come," he said.

"Oh God, please, yes," she breathed. "Take me back to the hotel."

"No. Here. Now," he said, pushing her dress up over her ass.

She startled, even though her hips ground towards him. "I can't," she said, wishing it weren't true. "Not here. I won't be able to—"

"You can and you will," he said, and pushed off the wall, dragging her over to the back of the low leather chair.

"No, you don't understand," she said, but he ignored her and pushed her against the chair. He stood right behind her, trapping her with her belly pressed against the dark leather, and let his hands roam all over her body. Stella felt herself gush, the wetness sliding between her thighs, and then she thought of the party outside, of all the people congregating out there, of Creighton—Creighton, who was sure to tell someone that something had happened. Any minute now, someone was sure to come through those doors...

"Sheikh Bashir, I don't think I can," she said. And then she moaned as he pulled her dress down, exposing both breasts. His hands were relentless, ruthless, pulling at her nipples and rolling the flesh between his fingers, mixing just enough pain with pleasure. But what if someone came in? What if…

"Bend over," he said into her ear.

What?

But Sheikh Bashir already had her dress bunched up in one hand, and he pushed her down over the edge of the chair, hard enough that Stella had to catch herself on the arms. She looked back over her shoulder, about to object.

"Look straight ahead," he ordered.

Stella hesitated. Then he thrust two fingers into her.

"Stella," he warned.

Oh God, she thought. *What is happening to me?*

Her body melted around the feeling of him inside her, and she was done, past being able to find the words to object. She gripped the armrests and held her head up, her entire awareness folding around the intrusion of his fingers. From somewhere far away, she thought she heard him chuckle.

"Good girl," he said.

He began to move his fingers inside her, around and around, slowly working her wider and wider. She was so eager for him that she felt her vagina open, and willed him in further. She wanted all of him. She no longer cared where they were; she wanted him to mount her right then and there.

She tried to say "please," but it only came

out as a mewl. Again, he chuckled.

"Then let us see how much you can take, Stella Spencer," he said, and he pushed another finger into her.

Stella gasped, but already she knew she wanted more, her ass angling up to him of its own accord, her leg lifting to spread for him and gain purchase on the back of the chair. He felt so *good*. She could already see her orgasm, like some distant, shining jewel, getting bigger and brighter all the time. His lazy strokes built it up to the point of bursting and then pulled back, again and again, until it seem to envelope her entire consciousness with the need to come.

"P-please," she said.

He lifted her left leg a little more against the chair, and steadied himself on the small of her back. He pulled out of her long enough to spread her wetness around—she was so wet, so wet—and she heard the tearing sound of plastic, and the cool spread of a lubricant, and then the tips of his fingers were back at her entrance, but all of them this time, pushing against her opening, forcing their way in.

"Unnhh," she moaned, and instinctively tried to pull away, even though there was nowhere to go; it was too much, too much. Her body threatened to shut down.

"No, Stella," he said behind her. "Relax."

And with his other hand he began to rub her

clit, pushing down and side to side with a gentle, insistent pressure, keeping to the rhythm of the twisting thrusts of his hand, pushing and straining against the walls of her entrance until...

Oh God...

The pleasure sparking through her from her clit to her pussy and back again pulsed to his rhythm, opening her wider, a little wider, with every beat, until finally he slipped all the way in and...

Oh GOD.

His entire hand was inside her, fingers curled in on themselves in a fist. She could feel every last, tiny movement, amplified until it was *all* she could feel. Everything else disappeared; she was full only of him, could feel only him, could only feel the orgasm he was giving her now slowly spreading over her, wrapping her in a dull glow instead of exploding from her core out to her limbs, her fingers, her toes. She had never felt anything like this before; it was like happy drowning.

And then he moved his hand.

He twisted it one way, then the other, and each movement sent little flashes of lightning through the cloud that enveloped her. Slowly, so slowly, he began to fuck her with his entire hand, and the cloud gathered, grew darker, and the pressure inside her was overwhelming.

When he rubbed her clit, the pressure broke.

Her whole body spasmed around his hand, starting from her vagina and spiraling out in an inexorable, violent wave of pleasure upon pleasure until her poor, overburdened mind went...

Completely.

Blank.

Stella had no idea how long it took her to come back to full consciousness. The usual period of blissful obliviousness, of fuzzy-headed happiness, seemed extended and stretched. Time wasn't quite the same. Her face, all over her face, it felt like pins and needles, but pleasurable instead of painful. She tried to move her head, tried to talk, but failed. It took her a long time to realize that she was nestled against the Sheikh's chest, her face pressed against his soft white shirt, her body cradled in his arms as he sat in the chair.

"Shhh," he said, and she felt his lips on her forehead.

For the first time in years, Stella Spencer was completely fulfilled. At peace.

Happy.

By the time Stella was able to speak coherently enough that Sheikh Bashir even considered moving her — and he insisted on carrying her, holding her tight against his chest, propriety be damned — the alumni event had clearly been over for a while. The catering company was busy clearing tables and stacking chafing dishes, and no one bothered to give them a second glance. They just assumed she'd had too much to drink.

No one in the world could have guessed that Stella Spencer had just had the most mind-altering, world-shattering orgasm of her life.

No one at all knows, she thought, looking up at Sheikh Bashir's strong profile. *Not even him.*

Stella had never been able to come like that with anyone, ever.

I am in serious trouble.

CHAPTER 10

Bashir watched the city streetlights strobe past on Stella's alabaster skin in something like a daze. They were moving aimlessly through the city in the back of Bashir's car, the driver having been given simple instructions: drive. Bashir needed to think, and he wanted to do it encased in this quiet cocoon while holding Stella in his arms.

He'd had only one moment away from Stella Spencer since he'd had his entire hand inside her, when he took a moment to wash up, and even that had been too long. That was, clearly, insane. And yet he had felt their separation acutely, like the pain from a puncture wound. He had thought only of her lips, the way her eyes still fluttered, of the sounds she'd muffled when biting down on that leather chair. He had actually missed her, in the space of two minutes.

Insane.

The act itself was not something he'd anticipated attempting with her, not over the course of a weekend, and certainly not in the library of the Alexandria Club. It was only some sort of perverse providence that he'd had a packet of lube in his suit coat. But in that moment, it had seemed the only thing to be done. She had needed something bigger than herself, something overwhelming, to clear a path through all the emotional detritus that littered her mind, and free her to feel the things she needed to feel. He had seen it, plain as day, on her face. All his years of study, his practice at the art of reading, hadn't left him with any doubt.

Yet it was all…out of sequence, was the only way he could think to put it. The extreme closeness that usually accompanied such an act was there, in a way—he felt it now, as her body relaxed into his, as her breathing slowed to match his own, as her thin fingers traced small, delicate patterns on the backs of his hands— and yet it was malformed, lopsided, incomplete. How much did he really know about her? He still did not know what had caused her such pain, and yet suddenly…

Suddenly…

He felt himself balanced on a precipice, on the verge of losing control completely. Perhaps he already had. Perhaps he had already fallen for this stranger. He had always meant to get inside her head, to give her a weekend of such intense pleasure that she would carry it with her for the rest of the life, taking his own pleasure as he pleased. He did *not* intend to need anything from her in return, besides her delicious body.

Bashir, he admonished himself. *Thinking of yourself again.*

"Stella," he said, craning his head down so he could see the lines of her cheek. She looked up slightly from where she sat comfortably on his lap, her eyes still languid, still relaxed, yet with that spark of fire that he so loved.

Love is a dangerous word, Bashir.

"Stella, are you all right?"

Worry crossed her face. Already it seemed her mind was returning to its usual hyperactive state. Bashir tried again.

"Would you like to go back to your suite?"

Now a flash of disappointment and hurt played across her eyes, but she remained silent, trying to frame her words. Clearly afraid to say no to him. Damn. Another miss. He was truly disconcerted. Perhaps she felt the imbalance, as well, and needed it to be restored. Bashir took a deep breath, determined to get it right, even if it required him to open up more than he thought wise.

"Would you like to see my favorite place in

New York?"

She sighed, relief and happiness flooding her face. "Yes," she said. "That sounds wonderful. I don't think I could quite get to sleep yet, anyway."

It was hard to tell in the sodium-tinged light from the street, but Bashir thought she blushed.

"So what is it?" she said, and put her hand casually on his chest. Bashir felt his cock stir once again, angry at all he had been denying it. Stella shifted her weight, burrowing her ass a little deeper into his lap, and he wanted to groan.

Is that a smile on her lips? Perhaps not so innocent, after all.

"You'll see," Bashir said, then laughed at her pout. "All right, a hint: it's famous the world over, but we'll be the only ones there at this hour."

"Do you get a special Sheikh pass?"

Grinning, Bashir puffed out his chest a bit. "As a matter of fact, I do. But this isn't a formal visit. No one will know. I prefer to visit this place as Bashir, not as a representative of Ras al Manas."

"Bashir has his tricks, too?"

Bashir raised his eyebrows, and slid a quick hand between her thighs, stopping with just enough distance to flick at her vulva. She inhaled sharply. "Sorry," she breathed.

"Sheikh."

"Much better." He squeezed her thigh, and felt his own body respond again. He wasn't sure how long he could keep himself from taking her, begging and true submission be damned. "An old friend of mine once helped the head of security at this place with a family matter, and he introduced me. I do have a special pass, as Bashir."

And then, for the first time in a long time, Bashir felt the presence of that old friend everywhere. Mark Kincaid. For a second it even overwhelmed his sense of Stella, striking a deep pain in his chest at the memories of his greatest failure, and of his long-dead friend. His only true friend.

The touch of Stella's hand on his cheek pulled Bashir back to the present. Startled, he looked down. Her face, still that curious combination of open and closed, of vulnerable and guarded, was a portrait of empathy. Sympathy. Caring. Genuine feeling. For the second time in a single night, Bashir was possessed of an impulse to go further than he thought wise.

"He was an old friend who passed away," he heard himself explain. "Mark Kincaid. He was my closest friend at Cambridge, and we used to attend those otherwise unbearable alumni functions together. This was the first time I'd been to one since his death, years ago."

"I'm sorry."

Her hand on his face was soft, yielding. Gentle. There was something primal about it; she asked nothing, only gave affection, and it made Bashir want to give it in return. And yet could he trust it? Could he really be that lucky? He had thought so once before, and his logical mind knew it would be foolish to think so again, and yet…

"I would have avoided it entirely," he said. "I would have preferred to spend the evening locked away in a room with you, but I had to catch Creighton at an informal gathering. I think that is why I was distracted. Why I made the mistake of leaving you alone."

He expected her to stiffen at his mention of Creighton, but she didn't. She continued to stroke his cheek, and the warmth and weight of her body pressed on him insistently, demanding his attention.

"It turned out ok," she said, smiling shyly.

Bashir burst out laughing. So it had.

She moved her hips, grinding into him, and unthinkingly Bashir reached for a plump breast. Her pleased sigh told him she had been angling for his touch; she was so close, so desirable, so demanding to be fucked good and hard. And then again, softly. And then again…

Bashir buried himself in a kiss. She was as sweet, as soft, as ever. He was sure he could get her to beg already. Why was his goal of her true submission, of her revelation of all her personal demons, so important to him? It was; it was deadly important. Bashir wanted nothing more than to bury himself to the hilt inside Stella Spencer, and yet he would not do it without submission.

Could it be that his obsession with control was misplaced? Yet the need to keep control, and the upper hand, in relationships had been a painful lesson to learn.

Could it be something he needed to unlearn? With her? A woman he barely knew?

"Stella," he said.

He never learned what he might have said next. His phone rang, with a distinctive chime. Only one number was assigned that ring tone, and there was only one reason they would call at this time of night. It was as though the universe knew he'd been speaking of Mark.

As gently as he could, he shifted a concerned-looking Stella off of his lap.

"Yes?" he answered. Then, not wanting to hear the details over the phone, he didn't let the caller respond. "Is it bad enough to come in?"

"I'm afraid it is, sir."

"All right. It will be a few minutes, I'm in the city."

Immediately tense, he leaned forward and rapped on the divider that separated them from the driver. The last thing Bashir wanted to do was take Stella to the site of *his* greatest wound, but he didn't have much choice.

"We will be making a detour," he said grimly.

CHAPTER 10

Bashir watched the city streetlights strobe past on Stella's alabaster skin in something like a daze. They were moving aimlessly through the city in the back of Bashir's car, the driver having been given simple instructions: drive. Bashir needed to think, and he wanted to do it encased in this quiet cocoon while holding Stella in his arms.

He'd had only one moment away from Stella Spencer since he'd had his entire hand inside her, when he took a moment to wash up, and even that had been too long. That was, clearly, insane. And yet he had felt their separation acutely, like the pain from a puncture wound. He had thought only of her lips, the way her eyes still fluttered, of the sounds she'd muffled when biting down on that leather chair. He had actually missed her, in the space of two minutes.

Insane.

The act itself was not something he'd anticipated attempting with her, not over the course of a weekend, and certainly not in the library of the Alexandria Club. It was only some sort of perverse providence that he'd had a packet of lube in his suit coat. But in that moment, it had seemed the only thing to be done. She had needed something bigger than herself, something overwhelming, to clear a path through all the emotional detritus that littered her mind, and free her to feel the things she needed to feel. He had seen it, plain as day, on her face. All his years of study, his practice at the art of reading, hadn't left him with any doubt.

Yet it was all…out of sequence, was the only way he could think to put it. The extreme closeness that usually accompanied such an act was there, in a way — he felt it now, as her body relaxed into his, as her breathing slowed to match his own, as her thin fingers traced small, delicate patterns on the backs of his hands — and yet it was malformed, lopsided, incomplete. How much did he really know about her? He still did not know what had caused her such pain, and yet suddenly…

Suddenly…

He felt himself balanced on a precipice, on the verge of losing control completely. Perhaps he already had. Perhaps he had already fallen for this stranger. He had always meant to get inside her head, to give her a weekend of such intense pleasure that she would carry it with her for the rest of the life, taking his own pleasure as he pleased. He did *not* intend to need anything from her in return, besides her delicious body.

Bashir, he admonished himself. *Thinking of yourself again.*

"Stella," he said, craning his head down so he could see the lines of her cheek. She looked up slightly from where she sat comfortably on his lap, her eyes still languid, still relaxed, yet with that spark of fire that he so loved.

Love is a dangerous word, Bashir.

"Stella, are you all right?"

Worry crossed her face. Already it seemed her mind was returning to its usual hyperactive state. Bashir tried again.

"Would you like to go back to your suite?"

Now a flash of disappointment and hurt played across her eyes, but she remained silent, trying to frame her words. Clearly afraid to say no to him. Damn. Another miss. He was truly disconcerted. Perhaps she felt the imbalance, as well, and needed it to be restored. Bashir took a deep breath, determined to get it right, even if it required him to open up more than he thought wise.

"Would you like to see my favorite place in

106

New York?"

She sighed, relief and happiness flooding her face. "Yes," she said. "That sounds wonderful. I don't think I could quite get to sleep yet, anyway."

It was hard to tell in the sodium-tinged light from the street, but Bashir thought she blushed.

"So what is it?" she said, and put her hand casually on his chest. Bashir felt his cock stir once again, angry at all he had been denying it. Stella shifted her weight, burrowing her ass a little deeper into his lap, and he wanted to groan.

Is that a smile on her lips? Perhaps not so innocent, after all.

"You'll see," Bashir said, then laughed at her pout. "All right, a hint: it's famous the world over, but we'll be the only ones there at this hour."

"Do you get a special Sheikh pass?"

Grinning, Bashir puffed out his chest a bit. "As a matter of fact, I do. But this isn't a formal visit. No one will know. I prefer to visit this place as Bashir, not as a representative of Ras al Manas."

"Bashir has his tricks, too?"

Bashir raised his eyebrows, and slid a quick hand between her thighs, stopping with just enough distance to flick at her vulva. She inhaled sharply. "Sorry," she breathed.

"Sheikh."

"Much better." He squeezed her thigh, and felt his own body respond again. He wasn't sure how long he could keep himself from taking her, begging and true submission be damned. "An old friend of mine once helped the head of security at this place with a family matter, and he introduced me. I do have a special pass, as Bashir."

And then, for the first time in a long time, Bashir felt the presence of that old friend everywhere. Mark Kincaid. For a second it even overwhelmed his sense of Stella, striking a deep pain in his chest at the memories of his greatest failure, and of his long-dead friend. His only true friend.

The touch of Stella's hand on his cheek pulled Bashir back to the present. Startled, he looked down. Her face, still that curious combination of open and closed, of vulnerable and guarded, was a portrait of empathy. Sympathy. Caring. Genuine feeling. For the second time in a single night, Bashir was possessed of an impulse to go further than he thought wise.

"He was an old friend who passed away," he heard himself explain. "Mark Kincaid. He was my closest friend at Cambridge, and we used to attend those otherwise unbearable alumni functions together. This was the first time I'd been to one since his death, years ago."

"I'm sorry."

Her hand on his face was soft, yielding. Gentle. There was something primal about it; she asked nothing, only gave affection, and it made Bashir want to give it in return. And yet could he trust it? Could he really be that lucky? He had thought so once before, and his logical mind knew it would be foolish to think so again, and yet...

"I would have avoided it entirely," he said. "I would have preferred to spend the evening locked away in a room with you, but I had to catch Creighton at an informal gathering. I think that is why I was distracted. Why I made the mistake of leaving you alone."

He expected her to stiffen at his mention of Creighton, but she didn't. She continued to stroke his cheek, and the warmth and weight of her body pressed on him insistently, demanding his attention.

"It turned out ok," she said, smiling shyly.

Bashir burst out laughing. So it had.

She moved her hips, grinding into him, and unthinkingly Bashir reached for a plump breast. Her pleased sigh told him she had been angling for his touch; she was so close, so desirable, so demanding to be fucked good and hard. And then again, softly. And then again...

Bashir buried himself in a kiss. She was as sweet, as soft, as ever. He was sure he could get her to beg already. Why was his goal of her true submission, of her revelation of all her personal demons, so important to him? It was; it was deadly important. Bashir wanted nothing more than to bury himself to the hilt inside Stella Spencer, and yet he would not do it without submission.

Could it be that his obsession with control was misplaced? Yet the need to keep control, and the upper hand, in relationships had been a painful lesson to learn.

Could it be something he needed to unlearn? With her? A woman he barely knew?

"Stella," he said.

He never learned what he might have said next. His phone rang, with a distinctive chime. Only one number was assigned that ring tone, and there was only one reason they would call at this time of night. It was as though the universe knew he'd been speaking of Mark.

As gently as he could, he shifted a concerned-looking Stella off of his lap.

"Yes?" he answered. Then, not wanting to hear the details over the phone, he didn't let the caller respond. "Is it bad enough to come in?"

"I'm afraid it is, sir."

"All right. It will be a few minutes, I'm in the city."

Immediately tense, he leaned forward and rapped on the divider that separated them from the driver. The last thing Bashir wanted to do was take Stella to the site of *his* greatest wound, but he didn't have much choice.

"We will be making a detour," he said grimly.

CHAPTER 11

Stella was going to have to learn to stay on her toes.

First, what had happened in that library, was just...there were no words. She still couldn't believe it. She couldn't even believe it was physically *possible*, let alone that she'd done it. That he'd done it to her. And that it had been so overwhelmingly powerful.

It had been like someone pressed her reset button. She'd come to, not as a blank slate, exactly, but somehow more open, more settled. As though the usual post-orgasm glow and sense of rightness with the world had just gone deeper into her soul.

Well, it had certainly gone deeper.

She could tell she would be sore, but it already felt like the good kind of sore, the kind you get from an incredible workout. Which wasn't entirely inaccurate.

She *still* couldn't believe it.

Even more incredible had been how close she'd felt to the man she knew as Sheikh Bashir. They had nothing in common, and yet she had never felt closer to a man as when he had carried her down to the waiting car. Well, she assumed they had nothing in common; she didn't actually know very much about him, as a person.

Which made this all so strange. And what made it so special when he'd offered to share his favorite place in the city. And when he'd mentioned his friend. There had been real pain on his face, pain that reminded her that behind the huge, imposing Dominant she had come to know, there was a real man.

A man she just might be falling for. Which freaked her out beyond anything she'd experienced so far. *It's just a weekend, Stella*, she thought. *Do not lose it. Don't let him in or you'll really be in trouble when the weekend is over and he decides to leave…*

That terrible thought had just crossed her mind when the Sheikh's phone rang. In a flash he'd gone from relaxed and sexy to rigid and grim, and where he'd seemed so close to her before, he now seemed a million miles away. Stella would have been hurt if it weren't so obvious that there was something else going on.

Well, she was a little hurt, anyway. A little concerned. Because the truth was that she wanted to be a part of this part of the Sheikh's life, too. She wanted to be able to comfort him, as he'd comforted her. To give something back.

Get a hold of yourself, Stella, that is nuts.

So she'd stayed silent as Sheikh Bashir had directed his driver to go to "Carthage House," wherever or whatever that was. She'd tried not to intrude as he retreated into his own shell in the back of the car, aware of the boundaries between them, and yet wanting to cross them with someone for the first time since her divorce.

They had left the city and the comforting orange glow of the streetlights a while ago, and were now driving through the black of some remote suburb. The darkness gave Stella an ounce of bravery, and she reached out to grab the Sheikh's hand. There was an awful moment when his hand lay still and she thought he might pull away, but then he squeezed her fingers in his own, and they sat like that, in silence, until the car turned into a nondescript drive.

Stella tried to get her bearings, but she couldn't see much out of the tinted windows.

There was a security gate, but they were waved right through, and the car drove back into blackness before turning into a brightly lit carport.

Stella gaped. She recognized this kind of driveway; even from inside the car, she could tell there was an ambulance bay. But this didn't look like a hospital. It looked like an old, ivy-covered Georgian mansion.

The car rolled to a halt, and she felt Sheikh Bashir retreat back into himself again. He released her hand, and got out of the car.

"Stay here," was all he said, and then the door closed with a firm, final crunch.

Stella watched his tall, broad frame walk purposefully toward the wide bay doors, saw that there was someone there to meet him.

Someone in a white coat.

Whatever it was, Sheikh Bashir was obviously upset. He hadn't retreated in anger; it had felt like the way a person retreats when they're hurt, when they need to hide away and tend to their wounds. Like an animal, in a way. It was something that was oh-so-familiar to Stella, having perfected it herself during the past few months, though now, looking at it from the other side, it seemed somehow obviously wrong-headed. Hiding away didn't accomplish anything when there was someone there who wanted to help.

And she wanted to help him, the way he

had helped her, even if he didn't know that he had. After all, in just the way he had pushed her to something she didn't know she needed, maybe he needed her to show that she wanted to be there for him.

Stella debated only a second longer, and then she opened the door and tumbled out of the car in a rush. She nearly ran to the doors the Sheikh had entered, afraid she wouldn't have the guts to keep going if she lost any momentum at all.

A heavy mist had condensed into a light drizzle, and Stella could feel her hair begin to frizz by the time she entered the stately looking building. She did her best to smooth it, and then remembered that she was wearing a likely ruined designer dress and heels, and no amount of hair-smoothing would make her look appropriate for the setting.

Which was exactly what she had thought it might be: some sort of expensive medical facility. There was no one at the reception desk, perhaps because they'd been called away for whatever it was Sheikh Bashir was dealing with. The lighting was different than it normally was in the hospitals Stella frequented for her volunteer work: softer, somehow more human. Soothing. The walls were a calming, happy shade of yellow, and the carpet under her feet was soft, yet firm, the kind that would absorb distressing sounds but remain easy to clean.

Stella was beginning to think she knew what kind of facility this was. It was the moneyed version of the sorts of places she'd volunteered in for most of her life.

She moved into the center of the foyer and looked down the hall to her right. It was a large building, probably easy to get lost in, but there was only one open door at the very end of the hall, streaming light into the dark corridor like a beacon. Stella walked toward it.

She heard Sheikh Bashir's voice as she approached, rumbling in a low, gentle murmur. It sounded like he was trying to soothe someone. Stella was stung by momentary regret: she was intruding on something private; there was no doubt about it. Yet, somehow, she felt it would betray everything she'd experienced so far with Sheikh Bashir if she were to turn away.

Slowly, quietly, she peeked around the edge of the doorframe.

Sheikh Bashir sat on a stool, hunched over a bed, speaking softly to an old, frightened woman. The woman's expression swung back and forth between confusion, fear, and recognition, even in the space of a few moments. The stress must have been incredible. She looked back at Sheikh Bashir as though she were about to cry.

"You don't talk to me that way!" she said,

her thin voice shaking with fury. "Who are you?"

"I'm Bashir, Ms. Kincaid," he said, taking her hand in his. "I'm a friend of Mark's. I'm here to help you."

The old woman snatched her hand away as though it had been burned, and slapped the Sheikh full in the face.

"I know *you*," she hissed at Sheikh Bashir. "You're no friend of Mark's. How could you do that to the boy? How could you?"

Holy crap, Stella thought. *What was that about?*

The Sheikh barely reacted, his voice never rising above that calm, soothing murmur. He was perfectly controlled, except for a hint of sadness in his eyes.

Or guilt.

But Stella didn't have time to ponder. The old woman pointed a crooked finger directly at her, and said, "Who is *she*?"

Slowly, Sheikh Bashir turned his head, as though he knew what he would see, and wanted to delay the inevitable as long as possible. His face, when he finally showed it, was twisted in fury. No, an attempt to conceal his fury. And betrayal. Shock. His face made it perfectly clear that this was much more of a violation than Stella knew. This was something she was never supposed to see.

Oh God, Stella thought. This was not what

she wanted. She wanted to help; she *knew*, specifically, in this situation, that she could help. She wanted to help both Ms. Kincaid and Sheikh Bashir. She wanted him to be happy to see her.

And now she wanted to know what he had done. What the man she felt she had grown to know, somehow, was capable of doing. What the man who had just been so deeply inside her could do to a person.

"What are you doing here?" he said, his voice cold. He was only keeping calm for the benefit of Ms. Kincaid—Stella was sure of it.

"I came to help," Stella said firmly.

Stella had never walked away from a frightened, hurting person in her entire life, and she wasn't going to start now. She'd do her best to help this poor woman, because that was what she did. After that, Sheikh Bashir could do whatever he wanted to her.

~ ~ ~

"Who are you?" Grandma Kincaid sounded desperate. Bashir had never stopped thinking of her that way, even if he'd learned to stop addressing her as 'Grandma Kincaid' because it upset her so. It pained him now to see her look back and forth between Stella and himself with such obvious fear in her watery blue eyes. She cried, "Where am I? Why can't I talk to

Mark?"

Bashir never knew how to answer that particular question. "Mark's dead" would be unspeakably cruel, but he found lying to Grandma Kincaid impossible. He never felt as inadequate, as helpless, as he did in the face of Grandma Kincaid's illness. All the money in the world at his disposal, and it did nothing to help him comfort this poor woman when she needed it most.

But apparently Stella Spencer knew what to do.

"Mark's wonderful, isn't he?" she said brightly, and picked up an afghan from the foot of the bed. She was so confident that Bashir himself almost believed that she had known his friend. He could only watch as Stella sat by Grandma Kincaid's side and wrapped her snugly in the afghan, holding the old woman close as though it were the most natural thing in the world.

Even more incredibly, it seemed to work. Grandma Kincaid began to relax into Stella's arms, swaddled tightly in the blanket.

"You're a friend of Mark's?" the old woman said hopefully, turning her face up to Stella's.

"Best looking boy at Cambridge," Stella smiled back at her, gently rubbing her back.

It's not a lie, Sheikh Bashir realized. But already Grandma Kincaid looked happier, as though she were relieved to find that she was among friends. Not knowing where you were or how you'd gotten there would be slightly less terrifying if you trusted the people you were with. Bashir himself knew that almost anything was tolerable if you had people you could trust.

It tore at his heart now to wonder if he could trust Stella. He had told her to stay in the car. It had obviously been a private matter, a serious matter, and then he'd looked up to find her spying on him.

Well, perhaps not spying. Perhaps that was a premature judgment. But no matter the outcome, Bashir had to face the fact that he *wanted* to be able to trust Stella Spencer, when, as a rule, he trusted no one.

And was that in any way a reasonable expectation, even for someone who was not in his position? To trust a woman he'd only just met, and under the most unorthodox of circumstances? Yet it was undeniably what his heart wanted. And now, watching Stella tend to someone she didn't know at all, watching her care for another human being in distress, simply because she could, Bashir felt comforted, too, just to know that Stella existed. Just to know that people like her truly, truly existed in this otherwise calculating, selfish, deceptive world.

If she were being truthful with him, that is. If this was who she truly was. It would break his heart, he realized, to discover that Stella Spencer had any other kind of motive.

Bashir recoiled from the hospital bed, clenching his fists with the effort to maintain control. *It would break my heart.* The phrase had entered his mind unbidden, because it was fundamentally, undeniably true.

This was a disaster.

Luckily—or not, depending upon how you looked at it—Bashir had spent a number of years learning how to tell when a woman was lying to him. He'd vowed it would never happen again, not after what it had cost him the last time.

He would have to rely on those skills now more than ever.

"Don't let him get fresh with you," Grandma Kincaid was saying to Stella in confidence. "He does have a way with the ladies."

"Who, Sheikh Bashir?"

Grandma Kincaid frowned. "No, dear. You stay away from *him* altogether."

Bashir grimaced, and then gritted his teeth when Stella looked up and saw his expression. He was supposed to be observing *her*, reading the micro expressions on her face, divining her intentions and desires, not the other way around. Even so, in the space of just a few minutes, he was sure Stella Spencer had learned more about him than any woman in his recent memory.

And Grandma Kincaid, as much as Bashir was ever devoted to her, was not helping.

Still, he had his responsibilities. This was clearly going to be one of those nights when his presence caused more harm for the old woman than good. He would do what he could for her elsewhere. Bashir bowed his head slightly and went in search of a doctor.

.

CHAPTER 12

Stella didn't know what to say. She could count on one hand the number of times she'd been left speechless in the twenty-nine years she'd lived prior to meeting Sheikh Bashir, and yet, in the two days that she'd known him, she'd lost count of how often she'd been totally flummoxed.

They sat together again in the back of the Sheikh's car—driving, she presumed, back to the hotel—only now, the distance between them felt immense. Insurmountable. She hadn't thought of it until now, but this was the first time they'd sat close enough to touch and...didn't.

Stella knew now that the boundary she'd crossed by poking her stupid nose into that hospital room had been much starker, much more inviolate, than she'd thought. And it wasn't hard to guess why, either: Sheikh Bashir had done something wrong. He'd hurt people he supposedly cared about.

Maybe that's what he didn't want her to know about. That wasn't such a terrible thing, Stella knew. It was only human. But that didn't make her feel any better about knowing there was *something*, while not knowing exactly how bad that something was.

But the very worst part was that she cared at all.

You lunatic, she thought, turning to glare out of the rain-splattered window. *He hasn't promised you anything beyond sex.* Stella cringed. *And money.*

She had completely and totally forgotten about the money. How powerful did her attraction to Sheikh Bashir have to be to make her forget about fifty thousand freaking dollars? No wonder he didn't trust her. He was *paying* her.

And yet she'd seen his face, watching her with Ms. Kincaid. That hadn't been the face of a man who regarded her with detachment. It hadn't been the face of someone who expected to say goodbye to her in just a few days' time.

Just thinking of it made her desire for him flare, igniting the memory of his touch on her body. *In* her body. She squirmed in her seat, wanting to feel her soreness, wanting to put pressure back on the beating pulse she felt between her legs.

Stella tried to figure out what to say the entire ride back to the hotel. She noted the growing height of the buildings outside with a kind of dread, knowing it meant they were closer to their destination, knowing, with some sort of gut certainty, that when they were no longer trapped in the small private world of the car, she would lose her chance to speak. She'd lose her chance to ask questions, to understand, to turn Sheikh Bashir back into the kind of man she wanted to be with.

Oh, hell, Stella. What does it matter if you want to be with him?

The fact was her head was swimming. Her vagina still throbbed with the feeling of him inside her, with the way he'd nearly turned her inside out and showed her a new side to herself, and now her mind was abuzz with anxiety and uncertainty about what kind of man he really was. And by the time she'd worked up the courage to open her mouth, the car had slowed to a halt.

"Sheikh—" she tried.

"Quiet," he said. He got out of the car, and held open the door for her.

Stella pursed her lips and promised herself that she wouldn't tear up, if only because she refused to appear ridiculous.

Sheikh Bashir led her through the lobby, deserted at this time of night, in total silence. He stayed silent all the way to the door of the suite he had booked for her, and then suddenly stopped. He put his hands on both her shoulders and turned her toward him, regarding her with an appraiser's eye. Then he quite suddenly pushed her back a few paces, until she stood fully in the soft light of a wall sconce.

"What—"

"I said *quiet*," he growled, and pushed her flat against the wall. The usual intensity of his stare was enhanced by a ferocity that Stella found genuinely frightening. "You will answer my questions, and only my questions, until I tell you otherwise."

His large hands burned into her shoulders. Stella couldn't help her physical response, even if her mind was afraid of disappointing the Sheikh, afraid of what he might say. She wanted to feel his hands everywhere.

She nodded.

"Why did you disobey my order to stay in the car?"

Oh crap. How to answer that without sounding like a crazy person? 'I thought I might be falling for you, and I had to check it out?' 'I wanted to know more about you?'

"I was curious," Stella said lamely.

Sheikh Bashir held her pinned against the wall with one hand, and thrust his other hand between her legs. The shock of his grip pulled a cry from her throat, and heat from her body.

126

"Let me remind you of our agreement," he said, his voice low. "You are *mine*, to do with as I will. You have disobeyed me. You will answer my questions now, fully and honestly, to the best of your ability, or by God, Stella, there *will* be consequences."

He held her frozen in his gaze, and it felt like there was nothing she could even think that would escape his notice. She could never lie to him. She hadn't meant to. Her only trouble was that his hand was making it difficult for her to think.

What is wrong with me that I want this? she thought. *That it feels so right.*

"Yes, Sheikh," she said. "I'm sorry. I didn't mean..."

But words failed her as he moved his hand. He finished her sentence for her: "To obfuscate."

"Yes. That."

"Then answer the question fully. Do not close your eyes. Look directly at me."

She did, and his dark eyes glittered. Again his intensity was...overwhelming. There was the definite sense that she was being studied, analyzed, x-rayed. In some sense it was comforting: she only had good intentions, and maybe he would see that.

"I wanted to know you," she said, her voice barely above a whisper. "It felt like you'd been so deep in me, so intimate, and I didn't know anything about you. I wanted to know what upset you, because I wanted to help. Like you've helped me. I wanted...I wanted to be closer to you."

There was a long pause. Finally the Sheikh swallowed, and spoke.

"And now?" he said. "After what you saw and heard?"

"I want to know more," she admitted. "I want to know why you feel so guilty. I want to know why you care for an old woman who hates you. I want...I want to know you, because I need to know..."

Oh God. Tell the truth.

"I've fallen for the wrong man before. I don't think I can handle doing it again."

There. She'd said it.

The muscles of the Sheikh's face froze. It didn't even seem like he was breathing. He studied her face for another impossibly long second, and then he took her mouth with his. His lips were swift, and hungry, and passionate, and it felt as though he kissed her with the strength of his own relief. As though he forgave her. And he pulled away before she'd had enough, leaving her dazed. It might never be enough. She was breathing hard.

He leaned his forehead against hers, and she heard him breathing, just as hard as she was. He sighed, then pulled away suddenly.

"Mark Kincaid was my greatest friend," he

said. His voice was artificially calm and studied, as though this was a speech that required special effort to say. He continued, "I trusted the wrong person, and Mark tried to warn me. But I was foolish, and ended our friendship instead. And then Mark died in a car accident, and I learned I'd been wrong. I also learned that there was no one to care for his grandmother. Since then I have assumed all responsibility for her care, even though she despises me, when she remembers me at all. I hope to find people who can make her happy, but even with unlimited resources, it is difficult. You helped her tonight, and for that, I am grateful."

He let her touch his face, tenderly, for just a short moment. Just a moment, in which she recognized that he felt it, too.

Then he grabbed Stella's arm and turned her around, pushing her face-first against the wall. Before she could speak or even gasp, he swatted her ass three times, hard.

"You disobeyed an order, Stella," he said into her ear. "And for that you must be punished, no matter how good your intentions. Your punishment will begin tomorrow morning. For tonight, you will have to suffer without my company. And with the knowledge that tomorrow is coming."

Stella's whole body clenched, her heart hammered in her chest, and all of the blood in

her body seemed to head downward.
   Tomorrow was coming.
   .

CHAPTER 13

Sheikh Bashir had been suffering an uncharacteristic bout of ambivalence since the previous night, when he'd given Stella the barest details of what had happened with Mark Kincaid. Why had he done that? He *never* revealed that sort of personal information, and he'd certainly been under no obligation to do so. But he'd read her face: she had been telling the truth. Every involuntary muscle twitch, every expression she didn't even know that she'd made, told him that she was truthful. Earnest. That she'd disobeyed him only with the best of intentions; that she hadn't done it out of malice, or some scheme to further her own interests at his expense, but that she'd done it out of…

No. Don't call it love. *She's known you two days, Bashir.*

Yet all of his training told him that she was

the genuine article. He couldn't help but wonder: if he'd learned these skills earlier, if he'd known them then, would Vanessa still have fooled him? Would he have been blinded by love, and been just as capable of being deceived? Had he been deceiving himself, thinking that with access to the best security firms and the latest research into micro expressions and body language, he could turn himself into a human lie detector? Was it a wasted effort, if he would still, in the end, have to operate on faith?

And yet he felt he had read Stella like a book. But not necessarily because of his skills: because she simply *was* genuine.

She'd been so vulnerable, admitting her motivations, and implicitly, her feelings for him, that he could not resist her. No, it wasn't even that; it's not as though she'd asked him for an explanation. He'd just known it would make her happy, in some small way, and he'd wanted to do that.

Get control of yourself, Bashir. Remember: she is here because you are paying her. That was the whole point, to keep things very separate, very clear...

And yet, he'd called his security firm as soon as he'd left her, the one he kept on retainer, and had requested a rush profile on one Stella Spencer. That was not the action of a man who was staying detached. Who was in control.

The dossier that had arrived by courier early that morning didn't tell him everything, especially not on such short notice. But perhaps enough to help him even the playing field. He'd revealed one of his most painful secrets the previous night, or at least most of it, and Stella Spencer, who was so instinctively genuine, was still hiding her most intimate, and possibly most painful, secrets from him. He could deduce most of what had happened with her ex-husband, but not the context that clearly made it so painful for her. And he needed to hear it from her. He wanted her to *want* to tell him everything.

He wanted her to truly, utterly submit.

Bashir turned the corner, and walked to the door of Stella's suite. He'd arranged for a wake-up call, and a delivery with specific instructions. He might not know everything about her, but he certainly knew enough to design a worthy punishment for her disobedience. He allowed himself a smile before becoming stern and foreboding.

And then he punched in the code, and opened the door.

Stella was perched on the edge of a three thousand dollar couch, dressed only in the slip dress he'd chosen for her. He nodded in approval; he could see every single on of her luscious curves, and even the suggestion of her nipples, through the thin fabric. She stood up quickly as he entered the room, and tried to smooth the dress, her expression apprehensive. Good. She should be nervous. He was going to take that exhibitionist streak she hid so well and bend it to his will.

"You are wearing nothing underneath?" he asked her. It was obvious that she wasn't, but he wanted to remind her of that fact.

She blushed. "Nothing, Sheikh."

"Show me."

A little hesitant, a little unsure. But obedient: she pulled up the hem of her dress, showing him her nakedness.

"Very good. Follow me."

He did not wait for her, but simply turned and walked out of the room, gratified to hear her stumbling steps trail after him.

Sheikh Bashir wondered if Stella had ever been to the Volare Black Brunch before in the course of her duties as a hostess. He doubted it. He'd never seen her there, and even employees who were not into the lifestyle were not welcome at such events. He smiled to think of her reaction. The idea of a BDSM brunch event had always struck Sheikh Bashir as the exact combination of ridiculous and sublime that Roman and Lola managed so well as Master and Mistress of Volare New York. Of course they would take a New York tradition like Sunday brunch and make it their own.

They arrived at the ornate black doors for

the second time in three days, and Sheikh Bashir held up his hand, bringing Stella up short.

"Have you ever been to the Black Brunch, Stella?"

"No, Sheikh."

"But you know what it is." She blushed again. He loved that. He'd see her grow redder than that before he was through.

"Yes, Sheikh."

He laughed. She was being very, very obedient this morning. "One more thing before we go inside, Stella. Put up your hair," he said, and retrieved a thin leash from his suit pocket.

Bashir watched Stella's reaction very closely. She stared at the leash at first, as though trying to confirm, repeatedly, what she truly saw, and what it meant. And then the blush slowly returned, starting at the top of her breasts, visible in the low-cut, flimsy dress, and rising inexorably to her lovely cheeks. Yes, she understood. And yes, she found it both arousing and humiliating.

Which was exactly the point.

"Stella," he warned, and she gathered her loose hair in her hands and lifted it off her neck. Bashir attached the thin collar, and it was done. He would be watching her, more closely than she could ever guess, to make sure this went exactly as planned.

"I should not have to remind you, Stella, but

proper etiquette is required here. You do not speak unless I permit it, or to use your safeword."

"Yes, Sheikh." Her voice was soft. Already her mind was preparing for subspace. Not for the first time, Bashir reflected on how amazing she was.

Then he reflected on what sort of expression she might make when she realized how many people she knew were about to see her like this. He smiled.

"Let's go, Stella."

CHAPTER 14

Stella's mind lurched about from one extreme to the other, never settling on any one feeling: hot, cold, humiliated. Hot. Horny. God, what was happening to her?

Sheikh Bashir opened the door, and Stella suddenly realized: she would know people in there. They would *see* her.

The thought sent her hurtling into an entirely new space, one in which all her concerns briefly fell away because they simply could not hold on, there was not room for them next to the screaming siren call that was her intense arousal and anxiety at the thought of being seen, like this, by people she knew.

She did not have time to reflect on any of this. Sheikh Bashir led her forward.

Why does this give me such a rush? she thought. Stella never expected that she might feel this way; she'd always had a million intellectual objections to this kind of thing, but she'd never bothered to try to understand how it might *feel*. And still, she didn't quite understand it, even as Sheikh Bashir was leading her on the end of a leash through the shallow twists and turns of the Black Room entryway. She didn't understand it; she just felt it. There was something about giving up such control, such sovereignty over herself and her body, that felt safe with him. More than safe. Thrilling.

They were almost through. Almost to the main room. Stella could here the clatter of cutlery, the clink of glasses, the laughter of people enjoying themselves at a lazy brunch.

The thought that they would all see her like this, that they would all know how much she wanted Sheikh Bashir, how much she craved his body and his approval, that it was enough to put a leash around her neck, enough to let him do anything he wanted to her…

Wet warmth pooled between her legs.

But it was terrifying, too. Humiliating. It was somehow *final* to admit these things publicly. Stella had never been at ease revealing her private thoughts; she'd always been terrible at hiding her emotions, and her one consolation had always been that she could at least keep her thoughts about those feelings to herself. But this would be like showing something very private to everyone who cared to look.

But Sheikh Bashir demanded it. It was like she had to reciprocate; she'd pierced the walls he'd built around himself the night before, and now hers had to come tumbling down too.

Sheikh Bashir paused just before the final turn, and looked her up and down. As though he were checking in, evaluating her state of mind. It reminded Stella of how safe she felt with him, no matter if it made sense. It gave a new flavor to the emotion coursing through her, taking the sharp edge off the fear and anxiety. Now she was only highly and tightly strung, a string stretched out almost to the breaking point, and vibrating only in anticipation of being plucked.

He smiled, and stepped out beyond the final partition, taking Stella with him.

"The Black Brunch," he said, and paused — whether so Stella could get a look at the room, or the room could get a look at her, she'd never know.

She'd never actually seen it before. The entire room had been transformed into an elegant dining room, with fine tablecloths and formal place settings, and servers clad in scraps of black leather bearing trays of bellinis and mimosas with quiet grace. There were a few scenes taking place, set apart from the main dining, almost as a kinky backdrop.

Stella was almost lost in the strangeness of it

when she saw the first person she recognized: Catie. At the bar, flirting with yet another employee that she knew oh so well—Jake, a Dom who normally worked security for the club. He looked to be filling in behind the bar. Both of them knew her, both of them were colleagues. And now both of them would witness whatever was about to happen.

My punishment. Oh God.

Somehow it had slipped Stella's mind, in the midst of all the new sensations she'd experienced in the last few minutes. But that was why they were here. Her punishment.

What is he going to do to me?

The thought echoed mercilessly in her mind as Sheikh Bashir led her into the dining area. Stella tried to ignore the eyes upon her, but it was impossible: she knew more than just her colleagues. These were the members of Volare New York, who she'd seen every day in her capacity as club hostess. She quickly realized she'd recognize every single face if she took the time to look.

Instead, she stared straight ahead, her eyes glassy and refusing to focus on anything but Sheikh Bashir.

The Sheikh led her to an unoccupied table for two, and, without thinking, Stella began to move around to the other available chair.

"No, pet." The Sheikh frowned, and pulled one of the heavy chairs back from the table.

"You will sit on my lap. I want access to your breasts."

Stella swallowed. Ok. She could handle this. She could more than handle this; she remembered how much she'd liked being fondled in front of Creighton.

Smiling, she sat on the Sheikh's lap. She giggled a little when he bounced her on his leg, shifting her weight.

The Sheikh reached up to grab one breast, and leaned his head into hers. "You did not think that this was it, did you, Stella?"

Stella shivered, even as her nipples puckered into hard little points, and her pussy grew heated. *What's next?*

"Hello, Bashir. A new plaything, I see?"

Oh, holy crap. Crap, crap, crap. That voice was unmistakable. Roman Casta. Master of Volare New York, and Stella's boss. Stella's *hot* boss. Roman had always been a little bit of a distraction, with this aquiline features and lean, hard body wrapped in a dark olive complexion. He'd never been on Stella's radar, really, but there was no denying that he was one gorgeous man.

One gorgeous man who was her employer, and who was watching her get fondled on the lap of a Sheikh.

"Stella, behave yourself," the Sheikh said. Stella realized she'd been hiding her face in Sheikh Bashir's chest. It was awkward, and somehow even less dignified. Bravely, she sat up, and faced Roman.

Roman, who was smiling.

"I have to admit, I didn't believe Lola when she told me," Roman said, grinning. "But it's about time."

"It was difficult to believe she'd never had a taste of the lifestyle, working here," the Sheikh said. "Particularly when she's so suited to it."

"Perhaps she just needed the right Dom, at the right time."

Stella's mind whirled into action. Roman knew more about her life than an employer strictly had a right to; she knew Lola had explained about the divorce as a condition of taking her on. Roman had agreed out of…pity? Empathy? Understanding? Stella still didn't know, but she knew that he'd been a perfect gentleman, never once asking uncomfortable questions, yet quietly observing her for signs of stress or unhappiness. He'd always respected her privacy and boundaries.

Until now.

Sheikh Bashir narrowed his eyes. It seemed to bother him that Roman was so familiar with her. With a start, Stella realized that Roman did, in fact, know more about her life than the Sheikh.

"What makes this the right time?" the Sheikh asked.

Roman shrugged, clearly not willing to go

into detail. He said, "All things need to ripen in their own time."

The Sheikh nodded, even though Stella sensed he was not quite satisfied. Roman's familiarity had somehow come between them, and challenged Sheikh Bashir's primacy as her...what? Her Dom? Her owner? As though reading her mind, the Sheikh reached inside her dress and pulled her naked breast out, reminding her that she was his. Stella gasped, and felt the familiar flush return as Sheikh Bashir rubbed his thumb over her aching nipple.

"And can she come right here? In public?" Roman asked, leaning back comfortably, as though getting ready to watch a show.

Oh God, please no. Stella was horrified. She insisted she was horrified; ignoring the rapid, wild pulse that pounded in her clit at the very thought. She couldn't do that. She couldn't. Furtively she looked around the room: Catie and Jake were still chatting at the bar, and Lola was working at the back, and there was Roman, watching her with that lazy, lupine smile, so obviously amused.

Sheikh Bashir's hand left her breast, leaving it exposed, and gently turned her face to his.

"She will, one day," he said seriously, and Stella's limbs suddenly felt like jelly. "She is not allowed to unless I command it."

His dark eyes searched hers, and once again

Stella had the overwhelming sensation of being studied, of being read, like an open book. Like everything she felt was put on display, even more than usual, and there was no point in trying to hide. The inevitability of it was somehow relaxing. After all, why put all that effort into concealment if Sheikh Bashir would see through it anyway?

It was freeing.

Slowly Sheikh Bashir moved his hand across her cheek, and ran his thumb over her bottom lip. On a stray impulse, Stella took it in her mouth. She wanted him, now more than ever.

He shook his head. "Don't think you're going to get out of it, pet."

Stella's belly coiled with tension. Sheikh Bashir looked back at Roman, smiling as though talking about a deceptive child.

"She's due a punishment, Roman. That's why we're here."

"Oh?"

Oh no, she thought. *It's coming*. What would he do? How could this get any more embarrassing?

"Stella, stand up," the Sheikh said.

Legs shaking, and not willing to look at Roman's laughing face, she did.

The Sheikh waved his hand. "Strip."

Stella breathed deeply. She should have known this was coming. What had seemed unthinkable only a few days earlier — the exact command she had refused the last time they were in this room—now seemed, incredibly, like something she could handle. Maybe. What was different now? But she knew what it was: it was the Sheikh. She wanted to please him, and knowing that it was what he desired erected some sort of barrier between them and the rest of the world, as though there were a glossy layer of protection allowing her to enjoy the humiliation, the vulnerability, the thrill, knowing it was all for *him*.

She shivered out of her slip dress, letting it fall to the floor.

Stella grabbed hold of that idea of a barrier and held tight; it was more difficult than she thought, standing there, stark naked, in front of Roman. In front of *everyone*. She felt hundreds of eyes on her, looking her up and down, appraising her, comparing her to other girls, matching the sight of her naked body up with their previous vision of a well-dressed, polite hostess.

Roman said, "Very nice."

The Sheikh laughed. "Oh, she's not done yet."

Icy little fingers danced up Stella's spine. The Sheikh pushed his chair out from the table, drawing the attention of the rest of the room. He gestured at his expansive, well-muscled lap.

"Over my knee, Stella."

Stella froze. She should have known this was coming, too. Of course it was. How could it be anything else? She couldn't say no, she couldn't safeword out—the idea of disappointing him, after everything they'd been through in such a short time, was unbearable. Worse, she didn't *want* to disappoint him. And there was the slight trouble of the butterflies in her stomach, and the heat in her core, and the certainty that she could feel her actual pulse all over her body...

She was turned on.

The idea of being bent over the Sheikh's knee, of the view she would present to all her colleagues and clients, of all those eyes upon her...

The Sheikh grabbed her wrist, yanking her out of her reverie, and pulled her forward sharply. "If I have to pull you down myself, Stella, I'll let Roman have a turn, too."

Stella was not ready for that, even if the thought made her even wetter. Roman's eyes twinkled, and Stella quickly leaned forward, attempting to lower herself with some sense of dignity. The Sheikh wasn't having that at all. Chuckling, he pulled her down so swiftly that she lost her balance. He caught her, manipulating her body with ease, his rough hands positioning and balancing her until it became clear that she would have no control over her body at all. Her legs kicked out behind her and her arms tried to find purchase on the ground until he laid an arm across her back and a hand on her backside, steadying her. Reminding her of just who was in charge. Her breasts hung over the side of his leg, pushed up on her chest, and her ass was in the air. She was entirely exposed.

There was scattered laughter, some clapping. It was impossible not to think about who had such a perfect view of her exposed pussy. Jake, at the bar. Certainly Roman. All of those members, all of her clients, all of the men that she'd have to see again and again when she hosted for the club.

It was beyond humiliating. Stella's mind wound around each and every one of those possibilities, those eventual further humiliations, building up both her anxiety and arousal in twin spirals, the blood rushing to her face and pussy, her pulse pounding in, her body crying out for release, and then, suddenly: he spanked her.

Sheikh Bashir spanked her again and again, each blow jolting her forward, setting her breasts swinging, every movement emphasizing how little control she had over her own body while splayed helplessly in his lap. She couldn't get away if she wanted to.

Only part of her wanted to.

He hit her again, harder, and she whimpered. She heard Roman laughing, imagined how cherry red her ass must already be. She did want to flee, to escape, to run and hide from this, but she was held fast. And she'd also never wanted the Sheikh more. She felt herself arch up to him, involuntarily, and her humiliation doubled.

Roman said dryly, "I'm not sure it's a punishment if she enjoys it."

Stella wanted to die. She'd at last had some comfort from the fact that maybe, just maybe, her pleasure itself was private. But they all must be able to see how wet she was. She could feel her juices spilling from her pussy, could tell her whole body was probably flushed and glistening with a thin sheen of sweat. She put her head down and closed her eyes, wanting to hide for the rest of her spanking.

The Sheikh was having none of it. He spanked her again, even harder, and then grabbed hold of her pussy with a rough hand. Stella's eyes flew open in alarm, and with his free hand he grabbed her by the chin, and turned her face partially towards Roman.

"Explain to Master Roman what you did wrong, Stella."

She tried to turn her head away, but the Sheikh had a firm hand. Suddenly he squeezed her pussy, and then spanked it. Stella heard herself squeal.

"Master Roman, I—I disobeyed an order,"

she said. She was nearly breathless.

"And?"

Sheikh Bashir spanked her again. Stella felt her whole body clench with the impact. Was it possible to come from something like this? She wouldn't have thought...

Oh please, I'm not allowed to come, don't let me come...

"And I violated the Sheikh's privacy," she panted.

He spanked her again, and this time the sound of flesh smacking against flesh filled the whole room. All other sounds had ceased. *Everyone must be watching.* The pressure in Stella's core grew just a little bit more.

"And will you do it again?"

"No!" She was so turned on, so close to the brink, she just wanted it to end. What if she came, in front of all of these people, without permission? What would he do to her? What kind of failure would that be?

"Why should I believe you, Stella?" He spanked her again, and then slid a finger inside her. "Faithfulness is important."

"I swear!" Stella shouted. She felt almost delirious with the effort of keeping her orgasm at bay as his finger moved inside of her. As everyone watched. "Please, I promise. Please, Sheikh, I'm so close, I don't want to disobey..."

At the last possible moment, he withdrew his finger, wiping it on her buttock. Stella whimpered slightly as he rubbed her back, easing her back down. But even as her looming orgasm faded, Stella's mind began to drain away, leaving her with just a sense of peace. As though all of her anxieties, all of her suffering, had melted in the heat of what had just happened, and now they were all just slipping slowly away, leaving nothing but the happy, blissful kernel of her being.

Whoa.

It felt totally and completely right. She felt free.

.

CHAPTER 15

Stella had no idea how long she laid like that, across the Sheikh's lap. When she finally began to pay attention, she noticed the sounds of brunch had resumed, though the Sheikh was still rubbing her back. She lifted her head slightly, and he caught her.

"Don't try to get up on your own, Stella," he said. "Let me help you."

He turned her over and scooped her up, holding her naked in his arms, and setting her down securely in his lap. She felt a gentle hand on her cheek.

"You did very well, Stella. I believe you will keep your promises, as I always keep mine."

Stella half-jerked awake, wanting to look into the Sheikh's eyes. That seemed *important*. His eyes were two black pools of utter calm. They looked the way she felt on the inside.

"Are you satisfied, Roman?" he said, not taking his eyes off of her.

Again, Roman laughed. "Oh, yes. No

concerns. Have fun."

Without another word, Sheikh Bashir stood, holding Stella as though she weighed nothing at all, and carried her over to a private corner booth. It hardly seemed to matter that she was still naked. It fit her mental state: raw, vulnerable, stripped of all artifice. Sheikh Bashir sat with care, wrapping her in his huge arms and holding her close. Stella's defenses were completely down. It was almost as if she didn't need them, cradled in his arms.

He stroked her body for a while, her cheek, her arms, her thigh, leaving her with a slight buzz that tingled over her skin. Finally, he said, "It was important to you that I came back for you, at the Alexandria Club."

Stella murmured, "No one ever comes back. They always just leave."

She'd said it without thinking, but her words penetrated the pleasant fog she'd been in since her spanking and woke her up. She couldn't *believe* she'd just said that. It was so starkly true, and so obviously a pathetic sentiment. She didn't want to sound pathetic. She didn't want to *be* pathetic.

"Shhh," the Sheikh said, and kissed her forehead, stroking her back to a state of calm. He seemed to know he'd veered close to dangerous territory, and now he went in a different direction. "You were very good with Ms. Kincaid," he said.

She sighed. "I volunteered with folks like her for a while."

"That work was important to you?"

"Very." She nodded into his chest.

"Why were you drawn to that, Stella?"

It seemed like such an innocent, easy question, that at first it didn't set any alarm bells off at all. But so close to what he'd just asked her, so close to what she'd just said about people leaving... Stella hadn't made the connection herself until he'd brought the two things side by side, but now it was there, indelible, undeniable. Of course there was a connection between her own shitty childhood and her desire to help people who had no one to care for them. It seemed so obvious.

Like he *knew*.

But it was just too big for her to wrap her mind around it. She didn't want to leave this happy moment and think about things like that.

The Sheikh's voice rumbled in his chest, gently prodding her along. "It was important to you, and yet you stopped?"

Stella yanked her head away from his chest, shaking it violently. She didn't want to think about that at *all*, let alone tell Sheikh Bashir about it. She never wanted to think about Robert and all the stupid crap he'd pulled after the divorce ever again, if she could help it. She knew that was foolish, but this weekend, just this weekend...

Sheikh Bashir pulled her back to him, hugging her tight.

"It's all right, Stella, nevermind. It's all right..."

It made no sense at all that a proper Sheikh, and a Dominant, no less, could be so comforting, and yet Stella felt herself melt into him. There was something about it that was so easy, so natural, as though he read her like a book, knew all her flaws, and still only wanted good things for her. It was intoxicating. Like getting drunk on happiness. On the feeling of being loved.

Oh, Stella, she thought. *Be careful...don't read too much into it...*

But she could already tell she'd ignore her own warning. She would let herself fall a little further, even though she was also beginning to understand that submitting to this man completely would involve telling him all the secrets she didn't even want to admit to herself. Stella wasn't quite sure she could do that, with anyone, ever again, and the idea made her sad.

Sheikh Bashir seemed to feel it in her body. He petted her hair, and said, "No, Stella, do not become overwhelmed. You are much stronger than you think. Look at what you did this morning. Rest now, and we'll continue with our day..."

Stella looked up into his eyes. "Continue?"

He smiled wickedly. "You didn't think this was all I had planned, did you?"

CHAPTER 16

Bashir couldn't believe there was so much joy to be had in watching someone sleep.

He'd carried Stella back to the suite while she was still half-submerged in a sort of haze after her experience at the Black Brunch, knowing that she would need to rest for a while. The intensity of the scene, of her involvement in it, and of the things he'd sensed afterwards while holding her in his arms...well, he'd felt it, too. They'd both needed time to recharge. So he'd carried her back, fully intending to hold her until she fell asleep.

But then he found he couldn't bring himself to leave.

He knew he should. He knew there were things he needed to attend to, phone calls to make, bridges to mend—particularly with the

Creighton family, who knew Cecil was an ass, but would still need to be mollified. But Stella had curled against his chest like a kitten, and her beautiful face had relaxed into the deepest peace, and suddenly it seemed as though there couldn't possibly be something important enough to tear him away. So he'd laid there with her, doing his best not to move or disturb her in any way, content to marvel at the depth of happiness to be found in such a simple pleasure.

The slight smile on her sleeping face gave her an expression of peaceful, gentle joy, and Bashir decided that this was probably her natural state. It contrasted painfully with the occasional twists of grief or sadness that he had observed when she spoke of her abandoned work with the elderly.

Or when she mentioned people leaving.

Both admissions were incredibly important; Bashir was certain that he'd have seen that even without all his specialized training in reading people. It was that obvious. *Great hearts come with great wounds*, he thought. His mother had said that often enough before she'd died, but Bashir had been too young to grasp its meaning, or to wonder why his own mother had had occasion to say it so often. What wound could have been so great as to make Stella afraid to do the work that she found most fulfilling?

Bashir could make only a rough guess. The rush report he'd commissioned on Stella Spencer gave the barest facts about her divorce and her upbringing, and Stella herself would have to fill in the gaps. If she wanted to, that is. Bashir wondered if she would believe how much they had in common, even coming from such different backgrounds. Absentee, uncaring fathers were apparently a universal problem.

She shifted against his chest, and let out a low sigh. He loathed to wake her, but he would have to soon if they were to take part in all the things that he'd planned for the day. The report on her past had been indispensable in the planning process. He was quite proud of himself for being so inventive on such short notice, but he had to be honest with himself about the purpose: he had planned a day of activities tailored specifically to Stella's hobbies and interests, but it wasn't just for her that he'd done it. It wasn't just to give her a fantastic day, not just to bring her to the point where she was comfortable enough to submit to him, to confide in him, to bring them both closer so that he might finally take her in the way she deserved. It was also for him. Quite plainly, he wanted to see her happy.

He wanted to see her come over and over and over again, of course, but he also wanted to see her simply…happy.

The realization had shaken him to his core.

He had thought, lying there with Stella sleeping in his arms, perhaps that was enough. *If all I get is one weekend where we may pretend at love before we must part, perhaps that is indeed enough.*

But immediately he had known that that was a lie. After the Black Brunch, with Stella lying against him, naked and beautiful and still smelling of her desire, it had tested the very limits of his self-control not to make love to her. For the first time, he'd let himself wonder why he'd put such restrictions on himself. Why, truly, had he demanded that she make such concessions, that she reveal all, submit completely, before he would take her?

Why is that still so important to me, when it started out as just another game?

Bashir feared that he knew the answer: that she already had hold of his heart, and that the best he could hope for was to even the playing field, to make sure that he could trust her fully, that his own vulnerability was at least reciprocated before they parted.

Must we part?

It had been an assumption. Perhaps one made out of defensiveness, but that did not make it an unreasonable assumption. Even if Stella proved to be everything he felt her to be, would she care for his kind of life? He did everything in his power to keep himself in the

New York sphere, managing the family business interests in the Americas, and he never intended to relocate to Ras al Manas. It no longer felt like home, if it ever truly had, and his responsibilities, such as they were, were here. Grandma Kincaid was here. He could not justify moving her or leaving her. No, he would be here, for a long while. But what about after that?

How would she fare at embassy events? Would she die of boredom? Or the false roles that she would have to play? He could not see her like that. He hated it himself.

But he was being foolish, incredibly foolish, to waste time thinking of these things that would never happen. If this weekend were all he would get, he would make it the best it could be.

He caressed her sleeping cheek. "Time to wake up, Stella Spencer."

He watched her come slowly to awareness. It was its own pleasure to see her remember the events of the morning, to see them replay themselves in her mind, projected onto her face.

Yes, she *had* enjoyed herself, and she wasn't quite sure what to make of that. Nor did she seem certain what to make of Roman's presence. That was the moment when pleasure turned to embarrassment on her beautiful face.

"Tell me," he commanded as he handed her the clothing he'd ordered for her.

"What?"

"Stella."

"God, it's like you're psychic. Fine." Adorably, she actually turned around to shed her bathrobe. "I was thinking about how I'm going to face Roman after this. And Lola. And, um, everyone else."

He heard the chagrin in her voice without even needing to see her face.

"Do you think they see what happened this morning as some sort of debasement?" he asked, moving close behind her. "As though it's something you should, in fact, be ashamed of?"

He smiled. He towered over her, and he could see the blush begin to crawl up her skin from over her shoulder.

"Maybe."

"Is that how you see it?"

"No. I don't know. I mean, objectively, if I were to describe it to someone..." She turned around to look up into his eyes, and the gesture slayed him. "But that's not how it felt, at the time."

"Everyone in that room this morning understands that what happened, happened on a deeper level," he said. "They've all partaken in something similar. They've all been to the space you enjoyed afterwards."

Now she looked down, her shoulders tensing. She was perhaps still tentative about the things she'd shared, or had almost shared, when in subspace. That was all right. These things took time.

"Finish getting dressed, Stella. We have places to be."

She looked at the t-shirt and jeans he'd given her, and then at his own informal attire, clearly perplexed. "Yeah, where exactly are you taking me?"

Bashir only smiled. She'd see.

The ride over was remarkable for how easy it was. As soon as his driver—ever a discreet man—closed the door, Stella had snuggled up to him, burrowing under his arm without a hint of self-consciousness or affectation. Bashir tried not to think about how natural it felt, or what she looked like under those jeans, or how seductive her scent was. He was a man unaccustomed to denying himself things, except as a matter of increasing his eventual pleasure. To do it because he might need to protect himself was anathema to him, and he felt the tension inside himself increasing with every passing second.

It had almost become unpleasant by the time they approached their destination. A road crew was repaving a section of 72nd Street, backing traffic up all the way to Columbus; with some relief, Bashir pressed the intercom button.

"Miguel, we'll get out here and walk. Come back for us at the prearranged time."

If Bashir had been looking for some reason not to fall further in...*something* with Stella Spencer, if he'd been looking for some blemish, some evidence of incompatibility, he was further denied as they walked together. Stella stopped at a blinking parking meter, regarding the beat up brown station wagon that was in danger of a parking ticket with concern. Bashir watched her pat down the jeans he'd provided for her, realizing too late that she had nothing besides what he'd given her.

"Do you have a quarter?" she asked.

Bewildered, he gave her the coin and watched her buy the brown station wagon a twenty-minute reprieve. Was anyone really that conscientious? That concerned with the welfare of people they'd never meet? Bashir didn't think he'd ever noticed a parking meter in his entire life.

She ran up to him, smiling brightly, and threaded her arm through his. "So are you gonna tell me where we're going?"

Bashir shook his head, and allowed himself a slow smile of his own. "Though I wanted to give certain parts of you a chance to rest and recover," he said, enjoying her now familiar blush. "I thought you might enjoy a different sort of physical activity."

And with that, he led her inside.

~ ~ ~

"A batting cage?" Stella said, understandably surprised to find an athletic facility underground on the Upper West Side of Manhattan. "A batting cage!"

She didn't know of any in the city besides the one at Chelsea Piers, and she was reluctant to go there, knowing how often Robert used the facilities. Didn't matter how vast they were; just the chance of running into him set her teeth on edge.

But apparently there was an actual batting cage hidden away uptown. It was bizarre. And it was the real deal. There were kids with families, young athletes, coaches — the works. The memories of her time playing softball flooded into her mind, filling her with warmth and with a competitive edge. She'd forgotten how good it felt to be really *good* at something. And she had been good; she'd been better than good — she'd been great. There was nothing quite so satisfying as connecting with a tricky pitch and knowing that you'd sent it flying farther than anyone thought you could. Hitting was one of the hardest things in sports, and Stella had been damned good at it.

Robert had basically refused to go to batting cages with her. He'd always insisted they do something he was better at, like squash, or golf, and in retrospect Stella realized it was because he just couldn't handle losing to a girl. He had really been that petty.

Probably should have been my first clue, she thought ruefully.

But now Sheikh Bashir had taken her to an actual batting cage. He'd teased her, and publicly spanked her almost to the point of orgasm, and he'd held her in a way that made her feel more cared for than she could ever remember rightly feeling, and now he'd taken her to a freaking *batting cage*.

'Thrilled' wasn't even the word. Stella was ecstatic.

"How did you know?" she asked as the Sheikh returned from the front desk bearing gloves and helmets. Even wearing a batting helmet, he looked amazing. His soft white polo shirt did nothing to hide his muscular chest and shoulders, and his arms, hefting various bats, rippled with tightly coiled cords of muscle. He still looked like he could command a room. Like he could command a legion, even in a polo shirt and jeans. Stella swallowed hard.

Focus, Stella!

"Seriously, how did you know?" she asked again.

The Sheikh turned towards her, his usually stern face a mask of mocking innocence.

"Whatever are you talking about?"

She punched his arm. "Come on. A batting cage? It was just a stroke of genius? Or are you *actually* psychic?"

She was only half-kidding. His ability to read her bordered on scary.

"I believe your impressive collegiate exploits are a matter of public record, Ms. Spencer," he said calmly, handing her a thirty-two inch bat, exactly the right size. "If one were so inclined to look."

Stella's stomach flipped over at least a few times. He'd cared to look her up? Just to see what kind of date she might enjoy?

Holy moly, is this a date?

When had her wild, impulsive, scandalous weekend as a paid submissive consort morphed into a wholesome, all-American courtship?

Well, not exactly a courtship in the strictly traditional sense. Her ass still stung a little from the morning's activities, and already her body was coming alive at the thought of what else Sheikh Bashir might decide to do to her.

Stella pressed her lips together, and tried not to look at his muscular arms.

"Do you even know how to hit, big guy?" she asked.

"I was hoping you might show me," he said seriously.

Was there anything not perfect about this

man?.

CHAPTER 17

CRACK!

Another solid line drive sent shooting off of Stella's bat. She almost hit the pitching machine with that one—again. She was breathing heavily and sweating, and she knew her hair was a mess under her helmet, and she was as happy as could be.

"You really are excellent at this!" Sheikh Bashir called from behind her. He was leaning into the protective netting, hands threaded into the mesh like every enraptured baseball player who'd ever watched her hit. Only the Sheikh's eyes seemed to flash and dance, and Stella couldn't help but wonder what else he was thinking about.

The red light came on, indicating this session was over. It was just as well—Stella could feel the soreness begin to take root in her arms and shoulders.

"I'm out of shape," she said, taking off her helmet and shaking out her hair.

Sheikh Bashir grabbed the waist of her jeans, his fingers brushing just below where her panties would have been if she'd been allowed to wear them, and pulled her to him for a hard, hungry kiss.

"You are the perfect shape," he said gruffly.

It was all Stella could do to maintain her composure. "Would you like me to show you how to hit?" she managed to say.

"Of course," he said, smiling. "It does not look so dissimilar to cricket, but I would love the help."

He moved past her, ready to take up position at the plate. She still didn't quite believe it. He seemed so...

"You're really ok with a woman showing you how to hit a baseball?" It was tough to keep the skepticism out of her voice.

Sheikh Bashir turned back around, his brow furrowed. "Why on earth wouldn't I be?" He seemed genuinely confused. "A man who feels less in such a situation would not be much of a man to begin with."

Stella gave a short laugh, thinking of her ex. "You're absolutely right," she said. "I'm sorry I even —"

"Don't worry yourself, Stella. Besides," he said, taking up his position at the plate again, "I would expect someone who is so thoughtful as to put change in other people's expired parking meters to be equally kind and thoughtful in all other arenas of life. I believe you will be a good teacher."

So he'd noticed that. She guessed it was sort of a weird thing to do in front of someone else, but it always made her feel good. Expired meters were the most random trigger memory for her, bringing her back immediately to a pretty ordinary day when her dawdling had made them late, and her stepdad had gotten a parking ticket. She still remembered putting her hands over her ears as he yelled at her, while her mom simply looked away. Not the best memory.

But what really struck her now, as an adult, was how perversely grateful she'd felt that her parents had even been paying attention to her. Stella suspected that her stepdad hadn't ever really wanted kids, though he'd convinced himself that he did long enough to marry her mom. For the most part, growing up, she was just left alone, as long as she wasn't any trouble. That day with the parking ticket, she'd actually relished the brief feeling that she'd mattered. When she'd told Robert that story, he'd looked at her with such undisguised pity that she'd immediately changed the subject. Ever since then, each quarter that she put into an expired meter was like a little prayer for other lonely kids, just a small attempt to add to the general goodwill in the universe. Stella knew it was silly, but she didn't care. It was the sort of private, personal ritual that she'd always expected to keep secret.

And she was wondering if she could actually explain that to another human being. No, not just to any human being—to Sheikh Bashir.

Wow. That was not like her. Not anymore.

"Stella?" the Sheikh said. He looked concerned. That just made it worse.

Get a grip, woman.

Luckily, Sheikh Bashir didn't need much instruction. From the way he moved it was obvious that he was a natural athlete, and whatever they did with cricket bats seemed to translate pretty readily to baseball. He took her few pointers on his form in stride, incorporating them into his swing flawlessly. She couldn't help but be impressed.

"You are actually looking pretty good," she said. "Just keep your eye on the ball."

He grinned. "Always."

Stella exited the cage and pushed the button. With a clank, the brand new pitching machine whirred to life. Stella had set it to sixty miles per hour in what she now realized was a sort of preemptive aggression; she'd so expected Sheikh Bashir to be a jerk about this, like every other guy, that she'd put the machine on the hardest setting just to teach him a lesson.

Whoops.

Sheikh Bashir jumped back, startled, as a baseball rocketed past him and bounced wildly off the back wall. He looked over his shoulder with a look, and then turned back and took his stance.

And hit the next ball.

Oh, wow. Maybe cricket was tougher than it sounded.

He punished fastball after fastball, the muscles in his back churning with explosive power with every swing. It was something to behold. Stella was feeling altogether inappropriate for a batting cage by the time Sheikh Bashir's session was over.

He took off his helmet, smoothing his long, dark hair with his wrist. There was a slight sexy slick of sweat on his forehead.

"How'd I do?" he said, smiling. But he wasn't talking to Stella. He was looking right next to her, and...down?

Stella looked to see a little red-haired girl of about eight standing next to her, clutching the cage just as Stella had been. Apparently Stella hadn't been the only one totally mesmerized by the Sheikh's performance, but Stella had been so engrossed that she hadn't even noticed the little girl appearing out of nowhere.

Good job.

"He's pretty good, huh?" Stella said. The girl nodded furiously. She was looking at the cage the way other kids looked at toys or Christmas presents. Stella recognized that look oh so well.

"Are you here with your family?" the Sheikh rumbled, closing the cage door behind him and squatting down to the girl's height. She shook her head, suddenly shy. "My name's Bashir," he said, and held out his hand.

The redheaded girl hesitated just a moment, then stuck her arm straight out. Sheikh Bashir laughed, and took her tiny hand in his.

"I'm Rebecca," she said.

"Are you here with a grown up?" Stella asked. Little kids wandering around on their own made her nervous. Someone should be watching out for this little girl.

"Over there," she said, scrunching up her nose and pointing to another cage. There was a single adult man and two preteen boys egging each other on. "They won't let me have a turn," she said. She sounded resigned, as though that was just the way it was and always would be.

Sheikh Bashir frowned. "Well, I will," he said. "And so will my friend, Stella. You know she was a champion softball player in college?"

The girl's eyes grew so wide Stella almost felt ashamed of herself. She wasn't famous or anything, she just played softball.

"Really?" the little girl asked.

"Want me to teach you how to hit?" Stella said. "You can go back and show up your brothers."

The girl's mischievous smile was priceless.

They spent a good twenty minutes with Rebecca, teaching her the basics. Sheikh Bashir lobbed gentle underhanded pitches while Stella helped her get her form down. By the end, she was swinging on her own and had knocked one or two into the Sheikh's shins, who grinned and bore it admirably. The only person who kept looking over her shoulder to see if Rebecca's dad had taken any notice that his little girl had wandered off was Stella. With each passing minute, she grew to hate the beer-bellied, baseball hat-wearing man in the other cage. Clearly Rebecca wasn't all that important to him.

Well, she should be important to someone, at least important enough to teach baseball to.

"Rebecca!"

Stella narrowed her eyes and waved to the man at the other end of the cages. He lumbered over, not comfortable with his middle-aged weight, with a slight frown on his face.

"Rebecca, it's time to leave. Come on," he said. He hadn't even introduced himself.

"I'm Stella," she said pointedly. "This is Bashir."

The man adjusted his hat. "Nice to meet you," he said finally. "Come on, Rebecca, we gotta get you kids back to your folks."

Without another word or so much as a

question, he led Rebecca back towards the front desk, where the two boys were already roughhousing. From where she stood Stella could tell that one of them—the one with the bright red hair—was probably Rebecca's brother, the other his friend.

"This may be unkind, or simply ignorant, as I have no children," Sheikh Bashir said behind her, "but I am glad that that man is not her father."

Stella laughed, surprised at her relief. "Yeah. I was just thinking that."

"Every child should be wanted," he said softly, and put a hand on her shoulder. Stella turned, mortally embarrassed that again he'd somehow read her thoughts, but for once, his eyes weren't studying her. They were looking into the distance, as though seeing the past.

Maybe there were some things Sheikh Bashir understood all on his own.

Impulsively, Stella hugged him, crushing herself against his chest. She wanted to smell the sweat of his exertion, wanted to feel the heat of the body that had so dominated her life the past few days, which had brought her such pleasure and such unexpected comfort.

"Are you all right?" he asked.

"I'm fine," she said into his chest.

He threaded his hand through her matted hair, and Stella remembered how very sweaty and gross she was. And she did not want to be that sweaty, gross chick with Sheikh Bashir. Maybe she wasn't totally ready to admit what she did want to be with Sheikh Bashir, but she knew it was not that.

"Um," she said, pulling back and doing her best to smooth her hair down, "does this place have showers or something?"

CHAPTER 18

Showers!

Just Bashir's luck that this place considered itself a proper gym with a proper locker room. As though it wasn't hard enough to control himself, to be away from her naked body, to know he *still* hadn't had her, now he had to contend with the idea of Stella Spencer soaping herself down in a shower just a few feet away?

It wasn't enough that this stupid date, his own brilliant idea, had done more to make him fall for her than vice versa. It wasn't enough that he had to watch her incredible body sweat while she proved what she could *do* with that body. Any normal man would immediately think of all the other things she might do with a body that athletic and that in tune with itself, and Bashir's sex drive, at least where Stella was concerned, was a few notches above normal.

And now she was showering.

Bashir paced the hall in front of the women's locker room like a caged animal, at war with his growing, demanding dick.

~ ~ ~

The showers were spare, but more than adequate. Stella felt better as soon as she stepped under the steaming stream of water, and it wasn't just because she'd felt all grimy. As soon as she had a few moments to herself, thoughts about that morning and her relationship with the Sheikh had crowded into her head. She hadn't really had a chance to process everything, not on her own.

Maybe that's not such a bad thing, though, she thought, soaping herself down. It meant that she hadn't had a chance to drive herself crazy with her usual series of what-ifs and rationalizations and doubts. The lack of downtime was forcing her to just plain *feel*, and what she felt under those circumstances continued to surprise her.

For example: the sore spot on her ass, when she ran a soapy hand over it, gave her goosebumps, even in a hot shower.

The memory of being bent over his knee, in *public*…and then the knowledge that, no matter how much heat built up between her legs, no matter how sensitive her breasts felt under the soapy suds, she wasn't allowed to come unless he demanded it, was enough to push all those worries right out of mind again.

The fact was, she'd enjoyed it. She'd enjoyed being punished, being spanked, in public. More than enjoyed it: it had been a catharsis. She'd never felt so peaceful, so right with the world, so emptied of all distress and worry, as when he'd held her, just after. Even if they had talked about uncomfortable things that maybe she wasn't sure she was ready for. Something about it had still felt right.

She'd never felt this sexy, or this desired. She'd never felt this *wanted*, which was strange, because he hadn't actually done it yet. He hadn't had sex with her. And yet every word he said, every move he made, made it perfectly clear that she was at the forefront of his thoughts, as though he wanted more than just her body.

It was a brand new feeling. She felt like a totally different woman.

It was that new woman who stepped out from the showers, with only a tiny, coarse towel held around her with one hand, just as Sheikh Bashir was closing the locker room door behind him.

Stupidly, Stella said, "This is the women's locker room!"

Sheikh Bashir stared at her, his dark eyes flaming. Then he locked the door.

"Drop the towel," he said. "*Now*."

Stella obeyed reflexively. Her mind didn't catch up to her body until the towel was already rumpled and useless at her feet. It was that Dom voice; it did something to her brain.

Why should she feel nervous about being naked in front of him? It wasn't like it was the first time. Yet Stella felt the blush begin on her fair skin, felt the familiar feeling of exposure, of thrilling vulnerability, of being on display for his pleasure.

Sheikh Bashir raked over her body with those molten eyes, leaving her feeling helpless before him. He didn't move, but even standing in the shadows, under the broken light at one end of the room, Stella could see that he was hard.

And he was huge.

"Lie back on the bench," he ordered. "Look at the ceiling. And spread your legs."

Moving slowly, and with an increasing sense of inadequacy, Stella looked around. The bench was a foot wide, plain, wooden. She bent to pick up the towel and spread it on the bench before perching on the edge. There, she hesitated.

She'd been exposed to the Sheikh, but never quite like this. Not under these lights, and not so...explicitly.

"*Now*, Stella," he growled, and Stella quickly lay back, her breasts falling slightly to the side, her eyes trained on the ceiling.

Was this how he would take her? Right here, on a bench, in a locker room? She wanted him more than anything, wanted to feel him on top of her, wanted to feel him driving inside her, again and again, but…like this?

God, yes, even like this she wanted him. She wanted him however he'd have her. With a great gulp of air, she spread her legs.

"Yes, Sheikh," she whispered.

And then she waited.

He didn't make a sound as he approached. The very next thing she felt were two massive hands on the undersides of her thighs, lifting her legs up and spreading them wider. She almost lifted her head, until she remembered his command to stare at the ceiling. Stella bit her lip instead, and waited.

She heard a low, guttural growl, an animal sound, and then there was a hot, wet mouth on her pussy, and she arched mindlessly to the ceiling. Stella grabbed hold of the bench beneath her, struggling to keep her balance, squirming against the Sheikh's hungry lips, but there was no release, no comfort—his hands held her firmly in place while his tongue licked her slit from one end to the other. Stella had never been totally comfortable with this; she'd never been completely at ease with being so open and vulnerable, but now she didn't have a choice.

The Sheikh probed her mercilessly, laving

her folds, working his way up to her clit. She whimpered at the unrelenting pressure, and yet he held her fast.

"Please," she said, her brain veering into dangerous territory, "please, it's too much…"

He sucked gently on her clit, and her moan betrayed her. She wanted to cry when he pulled his mouth away, and at the same time, she wanted to cross her legs and hide.

"I will do what I want," he said roughly, "and I want to make you thrash. You will come for me now, Stella."

He lifted one leg over his shoulder and spread the other wide, opening her even further. Stella whimpered again, and gripped the bench below even tighter. Her abdominals all bore down on her pussy, the tension sudden and straining, almost painful. She closed her eyes, and tried to ride the sensation as his lips wrapped around her clit.

He sucked on it, drawing it into his mouth and applying pressure with his tongue, and just when Stella thought she couldn't take more of such an otherworldly feeling, he slid two crooked fingers into her.

"Oh my God!" she burst out, and felt her legs begin to shake. The Sheikh bore down on her harder, more insistently, his mouth coaxing her clit to greater and greater heights and his fingers rubbing and pressing against her g-spot. Every nerve, every individual, jumping, live nerve in her body sung in harmony to what he did to her. All sensation drew down, and gathered, swollen, around the hot button inside of her, and for a horrible moment Stella felt like she had to pee. She raised her head and tried to shift, but the Sheikh pressed down now on her belly with his free hand, as though trying to make a bridge inside her from his fingers to his hand, and the swollen feeling exploded outward.

Stella felt like she was drowning in an ocean that came from her, from which waves welled up and crested from her core, flowing over and through her and obliterating everything in their path. Her boneless limbs flailed helplessly, and she might have fallen if the Sheikh's arms hadn't been there to steady her, to hold her, to catch her.

This time she came to still shuddering, still at the mercy of her own aftershocks. The Sheikh rose up between her legs and looked down at her shivering, naked body. Through the haze of aftermath, Stella could see one thing: he was still hard.

"Get dressed as soon as you are able," he said, his eyes never leaving her nakedness. "We have plans."

He turned to leave. Stella called out, "Wait!"

He paused, his hand on the door. "This once," he said, "I'll forgive the lack of decorum. What is it, Stella?"

She rose, and tried to cover herself, suddenly embarrassed. But it was now or never. She wouldn't feel so free, so relaxed, except after one of the Sheikh's massive orgasms.

"Why haven't you…" She couldn't look at him. "Why haven't you fucked me?"

There was a long pause. When he spoke, his voice was even, though with a trace of strain. A promise of something.

"Because you have yet to fully submit."

He left her there, to think about what that would mean. No, she knew what it meant. It meant giving up every part of herself. It meant telling him things…it meant being completely at his mercy. She wanted him more than anyone, more than anything, she'd ever wanted in her entire life. The possibility of never knowing what it would feel like to have him inside her, plunging ever deeper, claiming her in every possible way, was not something she wanted to contemplate.

But what if she wasn't able to submit? What if she just couldn't bring herself to be that open? To be that vulnerable?

What if Robert had damaged her so badly that she was simply…broken?

CHAPTER 19

Bashir wouldn't say that he was nervous. He would never use the word 'nervous.' It was a weak word, and the connotation was undeniably one of the anticipation of failure. Bashir did not anticipate failure, and he was not uncertain.

He was, instead, in a heightened state of awareness.

He remained silent during the drive to their destination, preferring instead to allow Stella's own sense of anticipation to grow to meet the enormity of the occasion, and to give himself a chance to admire her in the dress that he'd had delivered. A shimmering, silver affair, with a slit that reached nearly to her hip, showing off one beautiful leg. He could tell that she felt out of place in such finery, but she would thank him for it later.

That is, if she did not walk out on him.

He had consulted the investigative report that he'd had commissioned, and he'd interviewed Roman, but in the end he had relied on his own intuition. He'd made his choice of destination based on the facts, yes, but it was his instincts that told him the confrontation itself was necessary. And his instincts were never wrong.

Of course, just because it was necessary did not mean that it would go well.

Roman had only given him bare facts, unwilling to give insight or to speculate as to Stella's inner feelings, and that was as it should be. That was for Stella to reveal to Bashir herself. He could only hope that she would choose to do so.

Bashir restrained himself from touching her with great effort. His better angels were regrettably silent as he contemplated having her right there, in the car. If she chose instead to leave, this would be his last chance to know her body, to feel her luscious flesh quiver around his cock, to make her come, screaming, with him inside her. But these were not honorable thoughts. He blamed them on the dress, and turned to look out the window so that he would not be tempted further.

It was a pointless exercise. She reached out and grabbed his hand just as the car pulled up to the restaurant. It might have been a temptation too far, except for her reaction as the signature awning came into view.

"Is this where we're going?" she asked. Her voice was painfully small. Bashir steeled himself. He had not expected this to be nearly as hard on him as it was on her, but he felt her discomfort more acutely than he'd ever felt his own.

"Yes," he was all he said. He got out and held open the door for her, wondering how long it would take her to realize that this was all deliberate.

He led her the short steps across the dirty pavement, noting the tension in the lines of her body, the way she seemed to try to make herself look small, protected, unnoticeable. She was preparing herself to be hurt. It made him incredibly sad, especially when he thought about the joyful, lusty woman she had been only a few hours before, laid out on that locker room bench.

He hadn't been able to help himself. It was all he could do not to plunge into her. Bashir was proud of his self-control, and his ability to take the long view, but the sight of her, still pink from the shower, breasts trembling, legs spread...that had tested him. It had tested him sorely. But to take her like that would have ruined what he wanted to achieve later that night.

And he was very, *very* much looking forward to what he would do to her later.

Stella clutched onto his arm as the doorman held open the gilt doors, and it seemed to Bashir that it was an impulse, that she had been trying to manage on her own, but at the last second had needed the support. He gladly gave it, not wanting her to suffer needlessly, and only wishing he could offer more.

Rococo's was one of only a few three-star Michelin restaurants in New York City. Even in the so-called capital of the world, Michelin was famously stingy with their stars; Bashir rarely agreed with their assessments, but for cachet, or for impressing young women, one could not do better than a Michelin three-star. Anyway, it wasn't his type of place. The converted meatpacking plant had been transformed into a dizzying array of gold, silver, and glittering crystal; even the plates were gold-plated. Bashir did not like to judge such things, but only the newly rich thought that this was a good use of their money.

Which, of course, was why they were here.

"Are you all right?" he asked Stella. She was still clinging to his arm, looking furtively from side to side, her shoulders hunched nearly to her ears. He hated having to do this to her.

She smiled too widely, her eyes pained. "Of course," she said. "This place is very good."

Bashir took a step as the maître'd turned to show them to their table, but Stella's fingers dug into his arm, holding him back.

"But maybe it's kind of fancy?" she said, a note of desperation in her voice.

Bashir shook his head. *She is stronger than this,* he thought to himself. *She is stronger than she knows; I am certain of it.*

His voice had the deep timbre of command. "Come, Stella," he said, "Now."

Reluctantly, she complied, and as she stepped forward he bent down, his hand over hers on his arm, and whispered to her, "Nothing can hurt you while you're with me."

Her surprise — her confusion — was interrupted by the maître'd, who had a lengthy speech that Bashir was sure he was required to recite. It was tiresome. Instead Bashir insisted on helping Stella into her chair himself, unwilling to allow another man near her, and busied himself looking around for the reason he had made the reservation in the first place.

Ah. Over there.

Bashir felt himself relax a little, the way he always did when all the moving parts of a plan were finally set into inexorable motion. It would unfold now, as it needed to. It all depended upon her.

He noticed, as they sat there, that she studied the menu with unusual attention. Surely she already knew it. She would not use that as an excuse to ignore her surroundings.

"Stella, give me the menu," he said.

She had a pathetically hunted look as she

handed it over. He couldn't wait to change that.

"I do not want you distracted," he said firmly. "I will order for you. Take in your surroundings, Stella."

Stella didn't pretend to smile, but dutifully did as she was told. The process of gathering her strength in obedience to Bashir played beautifully across her face, and he felt himself grow hard under the table. Finally having her would be one of the greatest experiences of his life, he was sure of it.

It was only a minute or two before she looked in that direction, and her reaction was immediate. Her entire body went rigid, and Bashir watched her chest flutter shallowly as her breathing became rapid. A sheen of sweat actually appeared on her forehead and across the line of her collarbone, and Bashir worried she was actually having a panic attack. He stole a quick glance himself, and saw why.

The man he'd expected to find at this restaurant, at this table, was, in fact, not alone.

Bashir reached across the table and grabbed Stella's hand. "Look at me," he said. She didn't appear to hear him. "I said: look at me, Stella. That is an order."

Her head snapped forward at the familiar, dominant tone, and she blinked back tears. Bashir felt his own heart sink; this was excruciating. He squeezed her hand, and was relieved to feel her return the pressure. She was not totally panicked, then.

"You know that man," Bashir said.

She nodded, dabbing at her eyes with her free hand. Then awareness seemed to wash over her, and she looked at Bashir. She didn't pull her hand away, but Bashir imagined it went a little cold.

"You know who he is," she said. It wasn't a question.

Bashir nodded. "Yes. It is why I brought you here."

Now she tried to pull away, but he gripped her hand and held it fast. The table shook beneath them, and a tear streaked down her cheek.

"Why would you do that to me?" she said, her voice full of tears. "Why would you do that to anyone? Do you have any idea, *any* idea, what it's like to see him like this?"

"No, Stella, I do not," Bashir said seriously. "Please, tell me."

.

CHAPTER 20

Stella wanted to run. She had never wanted to run so badly in her entire life, not even when her family life had gotten really bad, not even when she'd been bullied in fourth grade, not even when she'd had to face the humiliation of being dumped the first time. And it wasn't as though she only wanted to run to get away; she felt she need to run to simply expel the energy, the rising grief and panic and hurt that threatened to bubble up inside her, like a big geyser of pain.

And Sheikh Bashir clasped her hand, holding her down like an anchor.

Sheikh Bashir had done this. It was suddenly so clear to her. He had unlimited resources, and had apparently done some kind of research. He'd orchestrated this. He'd brought her here for the singular purpose of making her see Robert Spencer, eating dinner at their old regular table, with another woman.

'Furious' did not begin to describe it.

She was furious that the Sheikh would put her in this position, furious that he'd obviously investigated her somehow, but mostly furious that, in the midst of this crazy, erotic fantasy that she'd been living for the past few days, now she was reminded of the very crappy reality that was her real life.

Because there was Robert, with his new life, and a new woman. They looked genuinely happy. She had a ring. A giant, flashy, gaudy ring. It was as though Stella had never even existed.

And now she had to explain this to Sheikh Bashir? It hadn't been perfectly clear to Stella until this moment how very much she needed what he had given her—a sense that she was special, that she was desirable, perhaps even lovable. And now she would have to tell him about being dumped? How Robert had left her?

It was worse than humiliating; it was frightening. Because when she told Sheikh Bashir, she knew what he would think, what any normal person would think, what everyone she knew did think already: that there must be something terribly, terribly wrong with her.

"Stella," the Sheikh said. His voice was gentle, and his thumb brushed over the top of her hand. She forced herself to look into his eyes, and saw there only a steady strength, an unyielding acceptance.

It was almost too much for her.

Almost.

"Stella," he said again. "Tell me. Now. If you refuse," he paused, almost imperceptibly, "if you refuse, you may leave, and you may keep the agreed upon fee in its entirety. But if you wish to stay in our arrangement for the remainder of the weekend, you must tell me now."

Stella didn't know what to say. Her mind reeled at the idea of walking away from Sheikh Bashir, of never seeing him again. She'd deluded herself into pretending she wouldn't inevitably had to do just that, but his words now — about their "arrangement," about the remainder of the weekend — reminded her with crushing finality.

And *the money*. Would he believe her if she told him that she hadn't thought about the money since the very beginning? That she didn't give a damn about it, not compared to him, not compared to everything he'd done for her, even if he didn't know it?

She didn't want her time with the Sheikh to end, but even worse was the idea that if she told him he might think differently of her. Seeing that same pity, that same repulsion in his eyes that she'd seen in so many others...it was like it would leak back through time, poisoning even her memories of their time together. She was afraid.

But she was also tired of being afraid. She had faced more than one terrifying prospect in the past few days at the insistence of the Sheikh, and she had surprised herself every single time. If she lost the Sheikh, too...well, she couldn't be afraid anymore.

Stella took a deep breath.

"Robert is my ex-husband," she said. "Though I think you know that. And that is apparently his new fiancée." Stella forced herself to look back over at what used to be their table to see the blonde flip her long hair with a laugh.

Really? she thought.

"The marriage ended badly," Sheikh Bashir prompted.

"The marriage ended as if it had never existed," Stella said, biting off the bitter words one by one. "I came home one day from a weekend at my sister's, and he was just gone. He'd moved all of his things out. He'd changed his cell phone number. There was a letter from his divorce attorney, but no note. There was *nothing.*"

Stella had to stop and swallow back a sob. What still got to her after all this time was the sheer contempt of it. He'd left her nothing because she was nothing. Less than nothing.

Not even worth a goodbye, let alone an explanation. How could you treat any human being like that, let alone one you claimed to once have loved?

"There has been no communication whatsoever?" Sheikh Bashir asked. His brow was furrowed, and Stella realized this was the first time she'd seen him look anything but completely certain. The disbelief in his eyes stabbed at her heart. She could guess what would come next: he would wonder why. It was so inconceivable that someone could do something like that that he'd wonder what she wasn't telling him. He'd think she must be crazy, that there must be something wrong with her...

Stella took another deep breath. It didn't matter. There was no going back now; she had to face the reality of her life.

"No. He just removed me from his life. As though we'd never even met, like I didn't even exist. He gave me the apartment in the settlement just so he wouldn't have to see me again. I can't even afford the taxes on it—he knows that. He just...erased me." She looked down at where their hands were still joined, wanting to take in the last image of them together before Sheikh Bashir knew her for the social leper she had become.

"I still don't know why," she said quietly.

Sheikh Bashir sat in silence. For a long time

Stella was afraid to look up, but when she finally did, she didn't see disgust, or repugnance, or the awkward distaste of someone who was re-evaluating all of their previously held opinions of her. His black eyes glowed like two angry furnaces, and the lines of his clenched jaw pulsed evenly.

"I know why, Stella," he finally said.

Oh, God, she thought. *Please just spare me this one thing.* What could he say? What did he see in her that made him think that he knew why Robert had left her like that? She dreaded to hear it, because she didn't think she could take feeling like that all over again: feeling that profoundly unlovable, that unattractive. That repulsive.

And yet, it would be a kind of relief, too, to finally *know*. Because the truth was that Stella had been driving herself absolutely insane trying to figure out what had happened, what she had done to deserve to be treated like that, why Robert had left her the way that he had. Her only reprieve had been Sheikh Bashir, and now that was ending. Maybe the Sheikh could give her some lasting relief by letting her know what was so wrong with her that people could leave her like that, again and again and again. Because there must be something. If her father could leave, if her step-father could care so little for her, if her husband could just cast her off without even a second thought...

She forced herself to speak. "You do?"

"Yes," he said, leaning forward, his hand hot over hers. "It is because he is a coward."

And his eyes flickered with rage as he looked over at Robert and his new fiancée.

"What?" Stella whispered. She couldn't quite believe what she had heard. She definitely couldn't make it fit with everything else she thought she knew about herself. She'd been so prepared to feel terrible again that she didn't know quite how to react.

"He could not face you because he is a coward," the Sheikh said fiercely. "And he left you because he is a fool."

The immense relief that Stella felt put such pressure on her heart, expanding through her like a giant balloon, that it forced tears from her eyes. *Dammit, do not become a blubbering mess.* She looked down, determined to control herself.

"Stella," the Sheikh said. "You must tell me how it can be that this is a surprise to you."

He was staring at her again, studying her with that characteristic intensity. She still didn't understand how he was able to just...see *through* her. There was no point in lying, or hiding.

"No one else has said that," she said. "They all just assume that I did something, that there's something wrong with me. No one will tell me what he says about me, but they've all drifted away. All my friends, except for Lola. They were all really his friends, I guess. It's not the first time I've felt like people just didn't want to have anything to do with me. At some point you have to wonder, you know? I've been thinking they must be right. There must be something that I just don't see. There must be something wrong with me, for people to keep leaving. It makes it really hard to trust anyone."

The Sheikh was silent. His face had become very stiff. God, she must be a mess. She was possessed by a stinging need to try explain, if only so she didn't sound completely and utterly nuts, and yet was sure that it was an impossible task. There was just no getting around it, and yet she had to try.

"It's not just Robert, ok? This stuff…I mean, my dad left, too, there's a lot of baggage around that. Oh God, I'm sorry," Stella said, wiping at her face, and wishing she could take her hand back from the Sheikh. Why did he hold on to it? "You can't possibly want to hear this. I don't know what you saw in me, back at Volare. I'm sure this isn't what you had in mind for the weekend, is it?" She laughed in spite of herself. "I just hadn't felt a man look at me like that in so long. It was like they could all sense that I was…broken."

Funny that the Sheikh, the man who saw through her more than anyone else ever had, couldn't tell how broken she was. *Life is just full of hilarious little jokes,* she thought.

"Is that why you worked with the elderly?" the Sheikh asked. "With people who had no one to care for them? Who were alone, or had been left?"

Wow. She hadn't expected anyone to figure that one out. She had only just figured it out herself.

"That hits a little close to home, yes," she whispered.

"Why did you stop?"

"Because I got the position through Robert. A college buddy of his ran the charity, and after the divorce…he decided it was awkward."

She looked back over at Robert and his date, only to see her ex give his new fiancée a piece of his food. It was like picking a scab, to watch them together. The truth was that she didn't miss Robert, not anymore. She just felt the wound he'd left her with.

"Stella." The Sheikh's voice cracked the air, and the impact of it forced Stella out of her miserable head and back into the moment. Startled, she trained her eyes on him.

He continued, "I guessed that there was something to make you feel that way about yourself. Rather, it was clear to me that you did feel such things, but the details of what had brought you to that point were unknown to me. Now they are. Luckily," he said, smiling devilishly, "I am prepared to deal with such inappropriate feelings."

"What?" She had never been so confused.

"You will no longer think like this," he said. "You will no longer feel these things about yourself, because you will learn to see yourself as you truly are. And you will begin tonight."

Stella's stomach did a few backflips. His voice had penetrated right to her core, turning her on, despite her emotions.

"I will?" she said.

The Sheikh reached into his coat pocket and placed a fine black box on the table. He still wouldn't let go of her hand. Instead, his thumb traced maddening patterns on her skin, reminding her of the power he had over her body. That old tunnel vision was returning, and it was becoming difficult to think about anything but the Sheikh. And his hands.

"Take that to the bathroom," he said. "Enter one of the stalls. Open the box. And follow the instructions inside."

.

CHAPTER 21

The Sheikh's voice still echoed in Stella's mind as she walked unsteadily to the ladies' room. He had used that tone again, that Dominant tone, and all of her obsessive, destructive thoughts had slipped right out of her head, leaving only room for sensation. She was riding the high of anticipation now, thinking about what it had felt like to be over his knee, and to be under his command.

She felt his eyes on her the whole way. It made her feel sexy, all over again. It made her feel wanted, even after she'd told him what had happened. It made her remember what he'd done to her just that day. The spanking, the locker room...

It was exactly what she needed. She didn't even realized she'd nearly walked by Robert and his fiancée until she was almost at the ladies' room, and then she didn't care. She'd shown Sheikh Bashir her greatest vulnerability, her greatest wound, and he'd actually helped to make it *better*.

Stella felt freaking invincible.

She walked into the ladies' room with her head held high and her hips rolling and the feeling that she was the sexiest woman in the building. Even the other women in the powder room, gathered around the mirrors like flocks of preening birds, all expensively dressed and delicately made up, even they noticed it. Heads turned to watch a proud, invulnerable Stella walk confidently past the wall of mirrors, down the long hall of doors leading to individual bathrooms, to the very last room at the end.

Stella closed the door behind her, and locked it. Then she took a deep breath, and opened the box.

Inside there was a note, resting atop…a toy.

Well, it wasn't a toy, exactly, except in the very adult sense of the word. *That is a vibrator*, Stella thought. *That is definitely a vibrator attached to a harness.*

She almost didn't even need to read the note. She did anyway, because Sheikh Bashir had told her to. And it was very, very clear: *put on the harness under your dress, insert the toy, and return to the dinner table.*

Return to the dinner table!

They were at a restaurant! There were other

people *everywhere*. And yet the idea excited her immensely, just knowing she'd be doing it for him. That he would know what she had done, and no one else would. That she would constantly feel so full of him, of his will, reminded that she belonged to him throughout the whole meal...

Stella inspected the vibrator more closely. It had one of those little pieces that jutted up to make contact with the clit, but, more importantly, it had a battery compartment. Stella could only hope she wouldn't accidentally set it off in the middle of dinner.

It wasn't hard to insert the toy. She was already wet just thinking about the Sheikh, and what he'd asked her to do. The harness fit neatly, leaving no lines under her dress, pressing the vibrator snugly against her clit.

Oh my.

This was going to be interesting. She felt pleasantly full, and every movement gave her a little thrill as the toy rubbed against her clit.

Walking back to the Sheikh was very fun, indeed. Each step sent little tendrils of pleasure shooting out from her clit to the rest of her body, ratcheting up the tension coiled around her pussy. She had one brief moment of panic, walking in the crowded, classy dining room, when she wondered if everyone could somehow tell by the way she walked. She stopped herself, and pulled it together. Even if she did walk funny, no one would guess "secret Domination sex toy" as the reason why. They'd just think she had uncomfortable shoes.

She was sure she was blushing, though. And she damned well knew she was smiling.

Sheikh Bashir looked her over with obvious satisfaction as she returned to the table. In her absence, a waiter had brought wine, and Stella gratefully took a big, long drink.

"Are you perhaps nervous?" the Sheikh asked, a twinkle in his eye.

"No," she lied. She shifted her weight, and the toy pressed hard against her g-spot. Stella sucked in a breath hard.

"It is specially designed," the Sheikh said lightly. He seemed not at all concerned with her growing embarrassment. If this got much worse, she realized, everyone really *would* know.

"Do you remember, Stella, what I told you when I first evaluated you?"

But Stella was distracted. She had, in a moment of weakness, glanced back to where Robert had been sitting, at their old table. It was vacant now. There was no trace of Robert or his date. Had she really been gone that long?

"Stella!"

Oops.

"Yes, Sheikh," she said.

"I asked you a question."

Stella thought hard—as hard as she could with the toy pressing against all her most sensitive nerves. "You said a lot of things," she said meekly.

He smiled indulgently. It made her nervous. Like he was planning something.

"Yes, I did," he said. "One of those things was that I would train you to come at my command. Do you remember that?"

Oh, God...

"Stella."

"Yes, Sheikh, I remember."

The waiter arrived, bearing plates of carefully deconstructed traditional *tapas*, whatever that meant. The waiter was older, a career server who likely made good money at a place like this, not an actor or something who was only biding his time. He was a professional. Which is probably why he did not comment when Stella suddenly sat bolt upright, gripping the edge of the table with both hands.

The toy had begun to vibrate.

The Sheikh was smiling.

Sheikh Bashir thanked the waiter, and, while the toy pulsed inside Stella, he grinned and briefly raised his hand to show that he held a tiny remote control. He moved his thumb, there was an audible click, and the vibrations intensified.

Stella squirmed, then quickly decided that

made it significantly worse. She looked at the Sheikh helplessly.

"Please," she said. "Not here."

"Exactly here."

He clicked the remote. Now the part pushed up against her clit started to hum, and Stella closed her eyes.

"Oh, no, Stella, you don't get to close your eyes," he said. Reluctantly, she opened them. "If you close your eyes again, believe me when I say your punishment will be severe. Do you understand?"

"Yes, but—"

Stella broke off and bowed her head, unable to finish her sentence without moaning.

"Look up, Stella. I need you to look around you. Look at all the men looking at you."

Stella pressed her lips together, afraid to make any sound at all, looking at the Sheikh imploringly. She couldn't imagine this really happening. She felt like she'd been swept away on a fast river, hurtling dangerously toward a roaring waterfall, and she was entirely powerless to stop it. She could feel the orgasm building in her pelvis, like a massive storm cloud gathering electric charge, waiting to unleash a violent torrent. Except she was in *a restaurant*.

The Sheikh had no pity. He gestured for her to look around. Stella was afraid of what he might do if she refused, so she steeled herself for the embarrassment, and looked up.

The first man she made eye contact with turned around, sure she was looking at someone else. The second made no attempt to disguise his hunger for her; he'd been watching her longer than she'd been watching him. The third looked at her with a sort of fascination, as though he couldn't quite figure out why he couldn't look away.

The heat was spreading over Stella's skin now, and she had begun to sweat. She looked back at the Sheikh, desperate.

"You can come silently, Stella," the Sheikh said. "I know you can, for me."

And he clicked the remote one more time.

"Come," he ordered.

Stella groaned, and her fingers dug into the tablecloth, rattling all their fine silverware, nearly toppling her wine glass. The first contraction seemed to last forever, expanding slowly outward like ripples in a pool. By the time it was over, she was panting, weak, barely able to sit up.

"Look around again, Stella," Sheikh Bashir said. "Do you see how every man in this place wants you? Some of the women, too. Every single one of them wants *you*. They are all jealous that I'm the one who gets to take you home," he said, smiling. "As they should be."

The incredible thing was, Stella believed him.

He made her come on command three more times before dinner was over, and with every instance, she began to understand just what his purpose was: to show her how desirable she was. To show her how wrong she'd been. To show her that she could stop thinking of herself as broken and unlovable.

Maybe even to show her that she was worth fighting for. As the Sheikh rose to give her his arm, Stella admitted to him how much easier the night had been for her once Robert left the restaurant. She didn't like that it was true, but she didn't feel right hiding it from Sheikh Bashir. She didn't exactly expect him to smile about it.

But he did.

The Sheikh said, "He was removed. Tonight was the last night that he will be granted admittance to this place."

"You can do that?" she'd asked, eyebrow raised.

"You can when you've bought the restaurant, yes."

Um, what? That seemed like kind of a big deal, and though Sheikh Bashir seemed completely unruffled, he also didn't quite meet her eyes as he said it. Stella knew better than to quiz him on it, but...well...he'd *bought the freaking restaurant*.

Which was maybe why, by the time they left, Stella couldn't help but wonder if even the

Sheikh could love her.

Is this the night? she wondered as the Sheikh escorted her to the car. She was still weak, still needed to lean on him heavily, and yet she hadn't been this giddy about a sexual encounter in...ever, actually. She hadn't even felt like this when she'd lost her virginity. In just a few days, actual sex with Sheikh Bashir had become...well, she didn't want to build it up too much, but it was true that she hadn't ever been with someone who she'd been so emotionally intimate with. Even with Robert, she realized, snuggled against the Sheikh's chest in the car, she hadn't ever really let him fully in. There had always been a protective wall.

The Sheikh had knocked down that wall without any apparent effort. He'd just bulldozed on through. And still she felt completely safe.

But when they finally arrived at Stella's now familiar suite, he didn't follow her in.

She didn't know what to say. She stood there, the door open, yet remaining a symbol a distance between them she hadn't known was there, and tried to think of how to get him inside.

"Good night, Stella," Sheikh Bashir said quietly.

"Wait!"

He cocked an eyebrow, and she

remembered her tone. "Haven't I..." she said, already hating how pathetic she sounded, "haven't I done enough? Haven't I submitted completely? I promise you...I'll beg."

Stella had never been so shocked by anything she'd ever said, and yet it was one hundred percent true.

He stood tall, filling her temporary doorway, and reached out to cup the side of her face in his large hand. He slipped his fingers into her hair, and grabbed it, just enough to jerk her head back slightly, and he captured her mouth with his. Her body flared at the suggestion of force, even after her exhausting night, and she whimpered when he pulled away.

"Almost, Stella," he said, a smile on his sensuous lips. "We'll see how you do tomorrow."

.

CHAPTER 22

Bashir was certain that he was losing his mind.

Where before he had only had an intellectual sympathy for addicts or the mentally ill, or anyone with an affliction that stole their will and left them at the mercy of some force outside of themselves, now he had an almost bitter empathy. No, not entirely bitter—he could never fully regard it as a negative thing. But he understood. He understood the passion, the near physical affliction, the build-up of a rudderless energy that threatened to consume all if it did not find release.

For him, Stella held the key to that release.

Obviously, he was already a madman. To walk away from her the previous night... He was actually still in awe that he had been able to do it. With every passing intimacy between them, every laugh, every erotic moment, every shared wound, his desire for her had grown. After her confession—and subsequent performance—at Rococo, it was now almost an intolerable, continuous torture. It reminded him a great deal of when he was a boy, when he had been caught spying on the serving women getting dressed, and his nanny had boxed his ears. He'd heard a high-pitched ringing for weeks. Nothing would soothe him.

Stella was worse.

The thought of having her, the way he knew he could, watching her voluntarily laying down every last defense, giving up each sensation, every thought, every scrap of will, to him...

He would settle for nothing less now, after all of this. That is, if he could hold out without going completely insane. Just the idea of what he'd planned for her made him instantly rock hard. Not so much execution of it as what it would represent for her, and, hopefully, for him.

It all made him feel slightly abuzz, on the edge of chaos, as though his skin were the only thing preventing the crazed, almost violent desire that swirled within him from leaking out into the world and causing havoc. Well, almost prevented it: he had *bought a restaurant*. Not a bad investment, actually, given the establishment, but not a particularly good one, either. It didn't matter; money was immaterial.

Of course, he hadn't bought it as an investment. He'd bought it, through his lawyer, on impulse — on impulse! Him! — at a cash price the owner chef simply could not refuse, just to take a jab at Stella's ex-husband. Just to preserve the Rococo restaurant as a place that Stella Spencer could still call her own, a place she could enjoy whenever she felt like it.

No, he obviously had gone insane some time ago, and was only just now realizing it.

And what if she took the money he had promised and decided never to see him again? Wasn't that the whole point of paying her, that she would not feel obligated? Or, he supposed, that her obligations would be very clear, very specific, very well delineated, and that he would know her motivations for a fact, and not have to rely solely on his training, on intuition, on the inconstancy of emotion? Didn't he want her to take the money and go back to her life, so that he might go back to his?

Only a few days ago, that had seemed a very rational plan. Now it was a complication that clouded the situation rather than clarified it. Bashir could not help but smile at the irony. *What was the old saying? 'When the gods wish to punish us, they answer our prayers.'*

Indeed.

He wanted to soothe every one of her wounds with the ways he wanted to care for her. He wanted to prove to her that she was not just worthy of adulation and love, but that she was probably more worthy than anyone else he had ever met. He couldn't necessarily have provided a cogent argument to this effect; it was just something he knew in his bones.

So, he thought grudgingly, pacing now in his own luxury suite, awaiting the hour he had appointed for her to be ready for him, *perhaps this is love, in its way.*

He stopped short. He'd thought it, the word. *Love*. The world had not come crashing down around him; his universe had not changed. And neither had his options.

Mark would have laughed until he cried, and then told him to go elope.

But those were larger questions, not necessarily suited to the moment, and Bashir would not let anything ruin this moment for her, or for himself. He made the executive decision that he would not think about it until absolutely necessary; it represented a dark thing on the horizon that he would eventually deal with, but he wouldn't let it impede upon this night. This night, when he would know if Stella Spencer—wounded, beautiful, sensitive, loving Stella Spencer—could trust him enough to inspire his own trust in her. It was all he could think about. All he cared about, to tell the truth.

Which, of course, led back to the conclusion

that he had completely lost his mind. Bashir sighed.

Everything was ready. He would know, soon, if Stella fully trusted him. In fact, everyone would know. Roman and Lola had confirmed the arrangements; the equipment would be available, and arranged as he'd requested.

As would the audience.

All that was left was Stella.

CHAPTER 23

This had easily, *easily* been the longest day of Stella's life.

She'd slept terribly, obviously, after the Sheikh had left her like that, warning her about "tomorrow." First, he hadn't...well, after all that, after everything she'd told him, and after she'd done everything he'd told her to do, it still wasn't enough? What did a girl have to *do* to get a billionaire Sheikh Dom to make love to her?

Even when he was paying her for the privilege?

She cringed. Well, theoretically, as far as he knew, he was paying her. She would *not* be accepting any money, she had decided on that. It would taint everything he had done for her if she did, and what he had given her was priceless, even if he didn't know it.

These past few days, she'd finally felt like

she understood what people meant when they talked about coming out of their shell. Or that cheesy butterfly metaphor, with the cocoon. Stella wanted to run around—admittedly, like a crazy person—and announce to all those people, no, you don't really know what it's like to emerge from a shell, to break free of a cocoon, to find yourself completely changed into someone you'd always hoped you could be, but *I do. Let me tell you about it!*

Stella hadn't ever thought of herself as the sort of person who could be confident of her place in the world, and, even more so, of what she might expect to get *back* from the world. She'd just sort of accepted that people wouldn't treat her well, and her job was to still be the best person she could be, under the circumstances. It wasn't really something she'd thought about consciously—she wasn't the self-pitying type, or at least tried not to be—but, looking back, it was clear her expectations were totally warped by that feeling of inevitable suckitude. When Robert had left, it had been completely heartbreaking, and, on some level, shocking, like a sucker punch to the gut. And yet, on another level, something deep and pitiful inside Stella had thought, *of course*.

The Sheikh had, somehow, miraculously, succeeded in getting that deep and pitiful thing to shut up. He'd sucker punched it right back, and Stella firmly believed that, no matter what happened, that deep and pitiful thing would stay dead. It was gone. She was free, forever.

Even if the Sheikh never wanted to see her again.

Maybe.

She had pretty much been unable to think about anything else, all day. What could he possibly have in store for her that she hadn't already done? And what if she failed? What if he decided that she wasn't really...

Well, what did he want from her, anyway? If it was just sex, well, he could have had that. He could have a *lot* of that, frankly. But the plain fact was that he hadn't had sex with her. So what else did he want?

Stella knew what she wanted the answer to that to be, but she didn't want to say it, not even to herself. It would be just like her, to screw herself over by falling for a man as unattainable in real life as Sheikh Bashir was. This was a fantasy weekend, not life. What did a Sheikh's life even consist of? The kind of man who bought a fancy restaurant on a freaking whim and thought nothing of it? She imagined his office with a giant map of the world, on which he'd manipulate little pieces, like a great game of Risk or something. It probably wasn't that far off.

How could she ever hope to fit into a life like that?

It was silly to even think about. And yet she was clearly doing just that, waiting for the usual dress delivery to arrive. She did have to wonder where they were going, and what fabulous dress he would have picked out for her to wear. She didn't mind getting a new designer dress every night, either, even if the Sheikh kept ruining them in ever more creative ways.

By the time the package and accompanying note did arrive—left, like all the others, at the foot of the door to her suite; she never did figure out who he'd hired to leave them— Stella had worked herself up into a state of nervous excitement. She felt buoyant and yet delicate, like whipped peaks of sugared cream.

It was a small parcel, actually. Much smaller than any of the others.

She opened it to find a note that said only "8pm, the Black Ball." And a collar.

Just a collar.

For the Black Ball.

Stella had to sit down for a while.

The Black Ball was the start of Volare NY's fall season, a massive costume party to welcome back the club's wealthy members from their summers in the Hamptons, timed for the very last night of the Labor Day weekend. Stella had never been. She hadn't worked at Volare NY that long, but she'd heard stories. This was the party where the BDSM elements of the club took precedence, and when even the most vanilla of Volare's members sometimes dipped into more exotic flavors.

She'd been nervous about the Black Ball back when she'd thought she'd just have to host. Now she was apparently attending.

In only a collar.

She'd taken all of her clothes off, somehow not any more accustomed to nudity than she'd been before all of this, and put the thin, soft, leather collar on. It snapped easily in the back, and there was an ominous metal ring in the front. She knew what that was for. She remembered the Black Brunch.

But maybe she'd misunderstood? She'd wrapped herself in one of the impossibly plush bathrobes that were in never-ending supply in the suite's bathroom, and waited for eight o'clock to arrive. She'd been naked at the brunch, it was true, but that was a punishment. Maybe he had something else in mind?

There was the telltale beep of the key code at the door. She was about to find out.

Sheikh Bashir strode into the room, looking, as he always did, incredible. Gone was the casual but impeccably tailored suit; in its place was a fine, loose white linen shirt, open nearly to the waist, and fitted black trousers. A man like Sheikh Bashir did not have to dress up for any occasion, if he didn't feel like it. And his choice of clothing seemed suited for...athleticism. Or ease of access.

Stella felt her heart jump at the thought. The sight of his tan skin, smoothed out over a well-developed chest and a hard range of abdominal muscles, did not help. She hadn't yet seen his body, had only felt it against her, through his clothes. It looked even better than she imagined. She felt weak.

Sheikh Bashir glowered at her. "Stand up," he commanded. "Why are you wearing that robe?"

"I—"

"Take it off."

That voice. Stella had an immediate, involuntary reaction to it now: her belly tightened, she got a little wet, even her nipples perked up. *He really has trained me,* she thought, and, marveling at the whole thing, happily did what she was told.

She *loved* being naked when he was clothed now. It made her feel nervous, and powerless, and yet so turned on.

Sheikh Bashir stepped close, close enough to almost touch the length of her. Stella sighed, and he held her face as he had the previous night, tilting it up toward his.

He said, "You trusted me with your innermost thoughts and feelings last night, Stella. Tonight, I ask you to trust me completely with your body. If you do…"

"…and then beg…" she whispered.

He smiled darkly. "Yes. And then beg."

He leaned down and kissed her, the heat of him burning through the last of her resistance and fear, stoking the fire in her core and spreading the warmth to every last, aching part of her. When he pulled away, she felt cold, and knew instinctively she'd do anything to get that warmth back.

She heard a *click*. Stella looked down, and saw that he'd attached the leash to her collar.

"Do you trust me?" he said, very quietly. She nodded. She did. Somehow, even though she was afraid, and nervous, she trusted him above all else.

"We shall see," he said. "You will have a special safeword for tonight, for this event. 'Rococo.'"

The name of the restaurant he'd bought. It seemed somehow fitting. Again, she nodded, and then leaned slightly into him, wanting to feel his body against her nakedness once more.

He allowed her this for just a moment. Then he turned on his heel, and led her toward the door.

CHAPTER 24

Stella wanted to laugh out loud, but from nervousness or absurdity, she couldn't tell. There definitely was something funny about waiting for an elevator while stark naked, with a leash and collar around her neck. Especially when they weren't alone.

Stella had balked a bit when Sheikh Bashir led her into the hotel corridor, until the Sheikh reminded her that Volare NY rented out the entire floor for the exclusive use of club members during the Black Ball. It still set her on edge, to stand and wait for an elevator in the nude. And then, of course, the others had arrived.

Another couple, the man dressed head to toe in black leathers, the woman wearing a very fine, very see-through mesh dress, waited with them for the elevator. The Sheikh had greeted them politely, calling the man

"Henry." Stella had no idea how she was supposed to act, so she ignored them. Or tried to. Henry had been staring at her naked body with obvious appreciation.

Henry was definitely handsome, in a preppy sort of way that didn't necessarily suit his dress, and well built. Even so, Stella might have found his attention creepy if it weren't for the presence of the Sheikh standing next to her. She must have moved closer to him, because as the elevator arrived, the Sheikh reached down and grabbed one buttock before giving it a light slap.

"Don't dawdle," he said, and, blushing, Stella trotted into the elevator.

But Henry was not to be dissuaded.

"So that's her," he finally said to the Sheikh, though he kept looking at Stella's breasts. *Wait, what has he heard about me?*

"Yes," the Sheikh said.

"Are they real?" Henry asked Sheikh Bashir. Stella blushed furiously. Yes, they were damned well real. "Mind if I see for myself?"

What? The Sheikh had made vague allusions to something like this, to the idea that she was a possession, to be loaned out if he felt like it, but only playfully. This guy Henry seemed to take it seriously. And while Stella didn't want anyone but Sheikh Bashir, the idea that she was his, to do with as he wanted...

She was turned on. She couldn't help it. The

idea of another man's hands on her, *at the Sheikh's orders*, was somehow...

Oh God.

She could tell, without even looking, that the Sheikh was studying her with that intense x-ray stare again. She was sure he could tell that she was turned on. He could always tell exactly what she was feeling. Exactly what she wanted. Stella just looked straight ahead, and pretended no one was talking about her.

"If you want," the Sheikh said slowly, and he took Stella's hand in his own.

The man called Henry reached out and cupped Stella's breast. Stella was too shocked to move, except to squeeze the Sheikh's hand. Henry grunted softly, hefting her breast, kneading it slowly. Stella looked at the Sheikh, ashamed at how wet she was, wanting somehow to tell Sheikh Bashir that it was only for him, but not knowing how. Sheikh Bashir's expression, as always, was unreadable, though when Henry began to toy with her nipple, the Sheikh's eyes flashed.

"That's enough," he said.

Henry immediately dropped his hand. "Lovely," was all he said.

Stella could feel the other woman's hatred from across the elevator. She was glad when the doors opened, and the Sheikh allowed the other couple to leave first. By the time the Sheikh led her to the doors of the Black Room, the other couple was nowhere in sight.

In fact, no one was. Shouldn't it be busy? Bustling, even?

The Sheikh stopped, holding up the end of the lead and signaling Stella to stop. All at once she desperately wanted to explain about the elevator, about how she wasn't really attracted to Henry, or to anyone else — which, wow, she really *didn't* want anyone else — she was just turned on by the *idea* of more than one man, as long as the man in charge was Sheikh Bashir. She opened her mouth, but the Sheikh put his hand over it, and looked into her eyes.

"Do you trust me?" he said again.

She nodded.

"I have been watching you, Stella. Studying you. And it is my responsibility to know you. Do you trust that I have done that? That I would only do what is best for you — for us — even if you yourself do not know what that is?"

He took his hand away so she could answer, but Stella was still speechless. He had said, "for us." Us. There was an "us."

She blinked, and nodded again. It was all she could do. Looking into her eyes, he ran his hand from her face to her neck to her breast, where he lingered, flicking the nipple with his thumb, and then down the front of her stomach, his light touch drawing her muscles into shuddering contractions, and then, finally, between her legs, where he held her sex in his hand. She felt he had tuned her naked body to its peak, and had primed her for whatever was in store.

What is he going to do to me?

"You are ready," he said, grabbing hold of the lead and opening the door.

She had no choice but to follow.

Both times she'd been to the Black Room with the Sheikh, she'd listened for sounds from the main room while they navigated the blind foyer. Those sounds had given her an hint, at least, of what to expect: the leather-on-flesh sound of a flogging, the clinking of metal and glass of brunch.

This time there was nothing: only silence. Stella's mind ran wild. She gripped blindly at the Sheikh's hand, looking for some reassurance.

And then, quite suddenly, they turned the corner.

The room was festooned with what looked like hundreds of real wax candles grouped in every kind of candelabra and placed strategically on every available surface of the room.

The very crowded room.

There was no other ornamentation but for the candles, and the crowd. They were silent, some with their champagne flutes raised, and watching Stella expectantly. They were also all clothed, some of them in fetish wear, others in black tie dress. Most were not masked, and Stella recognized many from her duties at the club. All of them were staring at her as she stood before them, naked. The only naked person in the room.

Which is why it took her a moment to notice the centerpiece.

On a raised platform in the center of the space, surrounded by candles, and with a heavy chandelier hanging above it, was the table she had remarked on the very first time she came to the Black Room with the Sheikh. The table with stirrups. With straps. With restraints.

"Come, Stella," the Sheikh said, and began to walk directly toward the table.

Stella almost didn't move, she was so transfixed by that table, by what might happen to her there. But a small storm brewed inside her, a familiar pressure, and just as the lead went tight against her collar, she found her feet moving forward.

No one else made a sound. She felt hundreds of eyes watching her as she clambered up onto the platform to stand beside Sheikh Bashir.

He looked down at her, and said again, "Trust me."

Then he raised his arm, and the silence among the crowd deepened. The weight of all of those eyes shifted to Sheikh Bashir, and Stella almost sagged in relief.

If she thought she had trouble being only *vulnerable* in public...

"Thank you all for providing me with this venue," he began. A few people in the crowd nodded. Stella thought she saw Roman out there, amid the members, raising his glass. *Of course they're all here. Are they all in on this?*

Sheikh Bashir continued, "As many of you know, Stella Spencer is employed at Volare New York as a hostess, but she had never participated in any club events prior to this weekend. She is now newly submissive. *My* submissive." Stella thought she saw a few raised eyebrows. Was he claiming her publicly? Why did he need to do that?

And did that mean that after the weekend...?

"But," the Sheikh went on, "there are a few things she has yet to do. I hope you'll all join in the festivities."

Wait, what? Join in the festivities? Like that guy in the elevator?

Stella didn't have a chance to ask any questions. Sheikh Bashir turned to her and said, "Get on the table."

Oh my God. It wasn't a surprise, except that the reality of it...to *actually* get on that table, naked, legs spread...

Stella hesitated only a second before Sheikh

Bashir's face told her that this was not negotiable. "Trust me," he'd said. And he'd known, somehow, everything she was feeling; he'd known her own limits better than she did, in some ways. And he'd always, *always* wanted good things for her.

She got up on the table.

"Lie back," he said, "and put your feet in the stirrups."

Stella shuddered, and was glad that when she laid down that she could only see slivers of faces through the candle flames that surrounded her. She closed her eyes, steeled herself, and raised first one and then the other leg into the stirrups.

She was spread.

She felt someone move between her legs as she opened them wide, only to find Sheikh Bashir strapping in one ankle and then the other. She was helpless now, entirely at his mercy. As if to make sure that she knew it, Sheikh Bashir thrust a finger into her.

She moaned.

"Look at me, Stella," he said. She looked down, between the shaking mounds of her breasts, to see his calm, steady face. "Trust me."

He moved his finger in a quick, wide circle, and she tried to clamp down on it in pleasure before he removed it. All she really wanted was him, she realized. She wanted him, and anything he wanted from her. She leaned her head back and felt herself relax.

"The blindfold," she heard him say from between her legs, and when she lifted her head to look at him, a thick, black blindfold was wrapped around her eyes.

Who did that? She felt the panic begin to rise a little, a reminder that there were other people here besides Sheikh Bashir, that she was doing this very much in public.

That she would undoubtedly do more, in public, before this was over.

"The arms," Sheikh Bashir said this time, and now there were sets of hands on either side of her, grabbing her arms and strapping them down on the table. Instinctively she struggled against them, inspiring some laughter from the crowd, though it didn't sound unsympathetic. She remembered the arrangement, remembered that she had a special safeword, remembered that, above all, he was Sheikh Bashir, and she forced herself to surrender.

She was now truly, completely helpless, with no choice but to trust in the Sheikh, and whatever he was about to do to her.

"This little submissive," Sheikh Bashir said, his voice booming, "does not believe she can come in public."

Stella heard a few boos and some disapproving tittering from the crowd. *But what if I really can't?*

"She has trouble, like many people, being vulnerable," Sheikh Bashir continued. "She has trouble because she believes she will be hurt, because she thinks she will be rejected. She thinks that anyone who sees her naked will not want to see her again."

She hadn't told him that. She hadn't even told *herself* that. And yet, lying there, naked, spread, and exposed, but blindfolded, knowing she was in public and yet protected from having to see other people watching, she felt the full wave of emotion break over her: he was right. He was absolutely, one hundred percent right.

And wasn't that the saddest thing?

Stella didn't *want* to be that person. Tears welled up in the corners of her eyes, and she willed herself not to cry. She would not pity herself. She was here to become different.

The Sheikh seemed to sense her struggle. She felt his warm hand slide between her legs again, just resting there, teasing her, and it drew all the distracting pain and pity out of her, leaving behind only the feeling of his hand, and the desire for more of it.

"We will prove her wrong," the Sheikh said to the crowd. There was an answering cheer.

A chill ran the length of Stella's entire body.

Suddenly she felt her legs begin to move. The stirrups were being moved up and out, opening her wider, bringing her thighs up toward her chest. She had thought she was exposed before, but now the view would be obscene. Sheikh Bashir could get at *all* of her this way, and Stella felt a quick spasm of fear. She'd only done anal stuff a few times with Robert, and it was never what anyone would have called 'successful'.

The Sheikh began to run his fingers up and down the length of her wet slit, probing the folds, dipping into her for more of her own lubricant. Stella's hips tried to move with him, but she was hampered by the restraints. She hungered for him; her *body* hungered for him. She moaned with frustration, fighting against the straps, and only remembered they were not alone when she heard more laughter.

Was it really so easy to forget? With the way his hands worked her, it might be. Already she was panting; already her skin felt too hot.

"Very wet," he announced.

Polite applause.

"The oil," he said next.

Warm oil dripped onto her nipples. It smelled of mint, and stung slightly wherever it spread. Just enough bite to feel very, very good.

But who —

Before she'd even finished the thought, there were hands on her breasts, rubbing the oil in, playing with her nipples, and it was very, very clear to her that they were not the hands of the Sheikh. They were acting on his direction, but they were not his. They were large, and rough, and male, and they seemed to like playing with her breasts very, very much.

Like Henry, she thought. Only it felt like there was more than one set of hands. How many men, at the Sheikh's command? Who was touching her?

Whose hands were on her pussy?

"The lube," she heard the Sheikh say, and the hand on her pussy pulled away.

Oh God, what...

Cold, thick lube dribbled onto her exposed anus. Stella let out a surprised yelp, and was rewarded with audience applause.

"Don't stay silent, Stella," the Sheikh said, his voice still coming, thankfully, from the region between her legs. "In fact, I won't let you stay silent. You will answer my questions — understood?"

Someone pinched her nipple, and Stella gasped. She hadn't answered quickly enough.

"Yes, Sheikh!"

Now a finger was spreading the lube around her asshole, working it into the tender flesh. She fervently hoped that was the Sheikh.

"This is very small, Stella, but it will feel very big," he said. "Much like the first time I made you strip naked before me; do you remember?"

Stella pressed her lips together, moaning as something probed against the delicate skin. She managed to nod. She was willing, she wanted so badly to show him that she was willing, but her body resisted the intrusion. She thought back to that first day, the first time she felt like the Sheikh had read her mind, and how he'd seen her fear, and after that it had been so much simpler to just...let...go...

She sighed, and something slipped into her ass, pushing past the tight ring with a *pop*. He was right: it felt huge. Filling. It felt simultaneously wrong and so right, like the physical embodiment of the forbidden. It pushed her arousal that much higher, keeping her now upon an almost impossible plateau, making her need for him, for an orgasm, that much more desperate.

"I remember," she said, and her voice already seemed strained.

She heard more laughter, and felt the Sheikh's hand on the underside of her left thigh.

"Very good, Stella," he said.

The hands on her breasts became more playful, rolling her nipples, massaging the flesh, pushing her ever higher. She already felt like she might pop. And yet the idea of coming in front of all those people...

She honestly didn't know if she could do it.

Some part of her clung to the idea that she would be safe, if only she refused to fully let go. It might feel terrible not to come, but at least it wouldn't be frightening.

Did she really believe that if they saw…?

She felt more of the cold lube fall onto the entrance of her vagina, and immediately her mind was right back in the present. Both at once? Could she?

"Stella," the Sheikh said, "relax."

And the bulbous tip of something large pressed against the entrance of her vagina. Reflexively, her muscles clenched, bearing down on the thing that was already inside her asshole, and she moaned. The hands and the oil on her chest never let up, straining the nerves of her nipples until they felt frayed and overheated, until she felt like they might actually be glowing. And each time she squirmed, the thing inside her moved against virgin nerves, filling her further. She was starting to feel sort of funny all over, as though the tingling mint oil was spreading, slowly, up the skin of her neck, towards her face and lips.

And she was so, so hot.

Two fingers pinched her clit, suddenly, briefly, and she yelped. And then Sheikh Bashir pushed something into her vagina with one long, hard stroke.

"Sheikh!"

Her lower body convulsed, shuddering and

banging against the metal table. She felt a hand — his hand, she was sure, large and familiar — on the flat of her lower belly, exerting a gentle but firm pressure, as though reining in her pleasure.

"Stay focused, Stella."

She did. She tried. She imagined it as a growing ball of light, all of the warring sensations around her body, all the different stimulus, gathering there, just behind her pulsing, aching clit. The feeling of fullness left little room for the rest of her, for any remaining anxieties or thoughts. It felt like if she stayed perfectly still, that growing ball of light would expand to envelope her entire body, and she might just float away into that nothingness of orgasm.

And then the thing in her ass began to vibrate.

Stella arched her back suddenly and violently; the hand on her stomach pushed her back down. There were calming voices coming from somewhere, but she barely heard them above the buzz of her own body.

The thing in her vagina began to vibrate, too, in an opposing rhythm, and though her body jerked back and forth, she was kept in place by the restraints and the hand on her stomach. She couldn't hold back any longer, hadn't realized until then that she was holding back. A frightening, animal moan started somewhere deep in her belly and tore out of her throat, until she was wailing unknown words.

The vibrator in her vagina began to fuck her. Someone moved it—in, out, in, out—in ever deepening strokes, angling it up until it hit her g-spot and sent her soaring. The glowing ball contracted rapidly, as though all of her being had gathered into a single point of infinite depth and density, and then, slowly, but with increasing speed, and with the inexorable, thundering pace of a not-to-be-messed-with force of nature, it blew her apart.

She screamed. Maybe she screamed. She wouldn't really know. She was pulled apart and outside of herself somehow, every particle of her spinning about in furious circles, dancing, fizzing, sparkling, until they came together again, somehow...rearranged. Different.

She reassembled, slowly, on that table, into a new, better version of Stella Spencer. She had come—come mightily—in public. Her body still shook, and her heart thudding in her chest was the loudest thing she could hear, and when she tried to speak, she found that her lips and tongue were somehow numb.

There was the sound of applause somewhere off in the distance. It didn't matter. Nothing in the world felt important anymore—not her worries, not her insecurities, not her fears — except for one thing: the Sheikh.

She tried to say his name, but couldn't. She felt hands releasing the restraints around her ankles and wrists and running up and down her limbs, warming them, working the soreness out of her joints. As soon as she could, she tried to sit up, only to find him already there, scooping her up in his arms from where he'd stood between her spread legs.

"I cannot wait any longer," he said into her ear, his voice choked and hoarse. "You are mine."

And he slipped his hands beneath her naked thighs, wrapping her legs around his waist, and lifted her effortlessly. She clung to his neck with all that remained of her strength, still blind, not caring to remove the blindfold, not caring to see. She only wanted to feel him against her, to smell his spicy sent, to hear those words, again and again and again: *'You are mine.'*

Her arms shook as he walked, still weak from that orgasm.

"Not long now, Stella," he said. He sounded so different. His voice was usually so smooth, so controlled — a precise instrument. Now it sound ragged and rough, unthinking and raw. She burrowed her face into his neck and felt him growl.

She heard the keycode, heard him kick open the door. So close.

He bent, lowered her onto the bed. She tried to rise, to help him, but his hand on her chest kept her down. She heard the rapid sound of a zipper, the rustle of clothing. Was he naked? She would need to see this, even if it meant delaying what she wanted most. Her hands moved to her blindfold, but his hands came down upon hers.

"Let me, Stella," he said, still with that catching voice.

She let her hands drop, sitting over the edge of the bed, blind and naked. He was still the Sheikh. She wouldn't want him any other way.

The blindfold fell away, and she blinked.

Oh God, there he is.

He stood before her, as naked as she was, dark skin shining in the soft light, muscles hard and yet fluid, rippling under that gorgeous, smooth skin. His cock was just as massive as she'd thought, the silken skin pulled taut over his swollen erection. It was nearly purple with pressure, with desire.

For her.

She looked up and saw those dark eyes burning bright in his face. Suddenly, ridiculously, she was nervous all over again.

"Lie back, Stella," he said softly. "And spread your legs for me."

Her limbs still trembling—from aftershocks or nervousness, she couldn't tell—she did as she was told, and looked up to find him studying her again. Somehow she felt more exposed than she had been in the Black Room, where an entire room of people that she knew had watched her come to the manipulations of double vibrators and unknown hands. And it was because he *saw* her. Saw how afraid she could get, saw the secret things she wanted, saw how hard she worked to protect herself. He had cared to look, and he truly saw her.

You cannot love until you can truly see...

She'd read that somewhere, years ago, and it had stuck with her, but she hadn't fully understood it until this moment.

He came forward and positioned himself between her legs, his hair falling forward over his forehead. She wanted him so badly, and yet, there was one thing...

"Wait," she said, hating herself. Hating this.

His head jerked up with a start. "Something is wrong?"

She closed her eyes, then forced herself to open them. She would be open as she did this, even if it frightened him away. Honest. Unafraid. She looked into his black eyes, and took one last leap.

"I don't want your money," she said. "I never...I don't...It was fun, it was a game, that's why I agreed. But now I could never take your money. I never want your money. I want—"

His eyes went soft, and he silenced her with

his lips over hers, a claiming kiss that he sealed with one, solid, full stroke, plunging the entire length of himself into her.

She cried out as he filled her completely. Her back arched into him, her legs wrapped around him, and together they rocked until he'd built her back up to that impossible peak, flying high above everything she'd ever known. He planted his hand by her head, lifting himself for leverage, and pulled out.

"Look at me," he said.

And he drove into her, hard and long and fast, again and again, stoking the burning heat that swirled around her center until it engulfed them both. She spasmed in shuddering contractions around his cock, drawing his own orgasm out, and he came, screaming her name.

Stella fell asleep with Sheikh Bashir still inside her. She felt loved, and cared for, and good enough that a man might choose to never leave her.

In the morning she woke up to an empty bed, and a check on the nightstand for fifty thousand dollars.

CHAPTER 25

Sheikh Bashir al Aziz bin Said awoke on the third morning of his incarceration, and grief filled his heart. He preferred anger. On the first morning, when he'd been tricked into leaving Stella asleep in the bed they had shared, he'd been arrested and brought to a supposedly fearsome jail called the Tombs, and there he had succumbed to anger. As his disbelief at his circumstances gave way, bit by bit, to towering rage, the police officers who had arrested and taunted him about the Tombs—saying that he might be big but he was pretty, and they'd just love him in the Tombs—had slowly fallen silent. By the time he was booked and processed, no one was making jokes.

That first day, he didn't speak after he'd been led out of the hotel in handcuffs, except to demand to see his lawyer and the Ambassador, afraid of what might happen if he let the anger surface. The response to his controlled inquiries was always the same. *'We called.'* *'There's some kind of mix up.'* *'Delays.'*

Bashir knew what this was all about. It was Creighton, furious about his humiliation at the Alexandria Club, calling in favors with an unsuspecting police captain. Creighton knew as well as Bashir did that nothing would stick, that nothing *could* stick: Bashir had diplomatic immunity. Even if he had done anything wrong, which of course he had not, it would be of no consequence. It was a privilege Bashir would never think to abuse, but after the first day had passed and it had become clear that Creighton was pulling in more than one favor, he had felt morally obligated to warn every officer that he came into contact with. *You will come to regret this. It will not go well for you. I tell you now, call the embassy, and do what you can to save your career.*

His pleas went unheeded. He did not envy any of these men when the Ambassador was informed. Worse, Creighton knew this. He knew he was sacrificing these men, and for what purpose? To annoy Bashir for a few days?

The bastard had guessed that the only way to lure him downstairs was to tell the police to say that the warrant was for Stella. That galled him more than the incarceration itself.

But what filled Bashir's heart with the

deepest grief was the knowledge that he had left Stella to wake, alone, and find the check he had made out the night before.

Why had he silenced her at that crucial moment? Did he think it had been romantic? No, he had thought he had all the time in the world to tell her he loved her. That, as improbable as it was, he believed he had loved her at first sight, but only now did he have the wisdom to stop fighting it.

Instead, he'd probably broken her heart. He'd implied she was a common whore. He hadn't even let her make her own confession.

He had been so certain of what she would say. Now…now he wasn't certain of anything. Had he ever known a man to make mistake like this, even if it wasn't his fault, and recover? Had there ever been such a hurtful, spiteful, pointless gesture? Had anyone ever wounded him as deeply as he had wounded Stella?

And after everything she had told him about her past. About the many men who had abandoned her. Well, he had bested them all.

He had worried about Grandma Kincaid, as well, and for one delirious moment, he thought, *well, if anything happens, Stella can look after her*. And then he remembered that Stella did not know where he was, that Stella probably hated his very soul, and that no one at Carthage House would know how to contact

Stella, because no one in Sheikh Bashir's life knew that she had become so important to him so quickly.

He'd punched the crumbling stone wall , then, in a stupid fit of rage. He hadn't broken his hand, but his knuckles looked well the worse for wear. It was just as well. No one — not any of the hardened criminals around him — had dared to bother him. Bashir guessed that the sheer malevolence and animal frustration he felt radiating from him in thick, dangerous waves. No sane man provoked even a tiny weakling in that state, let alone a man of Bashir's size and strength.

It was on the third day that an extremely worried looking corrections officer came to collect him.

Bashir sighed. Finally. "I am being released?"

"Yes, sir." The officer wouldn't even look at him. He wasn't one of the ones who'd tried to frighten him, but even this poor fat little man might feel the sting of the repercussions, simply for being in the vicinity.

"Tell me your name," Bashir said to him, "and I'll mention that you were kind."

The fat little man had stayed silent, debating whether to speak, until the last gate had been opened and Bashir could see the enraged face of the Ambassador on the other side of some bulletproof glass.

"Granger, sir," the fat little man said hurriedly. "My name's Granger. They didn't mean it, honestly. You didn't have your identification, and..." He swallowed, seemingly with a distaste for excuses. Finally he simply explained. "They were just doing what they thought they had to do, sir."

In spite of himself, Sheikh Bashir laughed. "That is my problem, too, Officer Granger. That is my problem, too."

But this was progress. He was free. The Ambassador would want to debrief him, would want names, an explanation. But that would all have to wait.

He had to find Stella.

.

CHAPTER 26

"Thanks, Lenny."

"No problem, Ms. Spencer," the gruff doorman said as he carried in a bag of groceries. "You sure this'll be enough for you?"

She nodded, smiling at the older man's fatherly instincts. He'd always told her that she reminded him of his daughter. "I'll only be around a few more days."

Lenny had been a lifesaver. He'd done more than keep out unwanted guests; he'd made sure Stella didn't have to deal with anyone at all while she tried to figure out how to reassemble the pieces of her broken life. He'd even picked up a disposable cell phone for her when he noticed that she refused to turn on her phone and that the landline had been unplugged.

"Just in case," he'd said.

It had come in handy. Stella had wallowed for a day, and then she'd come to a decision. A series of decisions, really. She'd sent her resignation letter to Volare, then she'd used the disposable phone to make a few necessary phone calls, and then she'd sent that horrible check to the Ras al Manas embassy.

It wasn't that Sheikh Bashir had broken her. It was that he'd illuminated for her how she was already broken, and that showed her what she needed to do to fix it. She hadn't been living her own life in New York; she'd been living Robert's. And she hadn't gone about building a real life for herself since the divorce. She'd just been in a holding pattern. Well, that was going to change.

Stella quelled a pang of anger and rummaged through the bag for the ice cream she knew Lenny wouldn't have forgotten. She laughed. Nope, he hadn't forgotten: there were three different flavors. She grabbed a pint of cookie dough and went hunting for a spoon.

But even cookie dough couldn't make her forget Sheikh Bashir. It would be easier if her body didn't still crave him. It was humiliating, really, how much she still wanted him, and ice cream was a poor substitute. And as much as he'd hurt her—which was enough to literally take her breath away every time she thought about it—as much damage as he'd done, he'd still managed to succeed at one thing, despite his eventual epic villainy: he'd convinced her that these relationship disasters weren't really her fault.

Well, they were her fault in the sense that she kept picking losers. But there wasn't anything actually wrong with her — she knew that now. Even if Sheikh Bashir did turn out to be a bastard, he was a useful one.

Stella just wished she believed he really was a bastard, through and through. He had behaved like one, obviously, but that just didn't jibe with everything else she knew about him. No matter which way Stella turned it around in her mind, she couldn't reconcile what he had done with who he had been to her.

And you never will, she told herself. *Sometimes things just don't make sense, and there's nothing you can do about it.*

So instead, she'd made a plan. No more relying on men. No more relying on love. And no more New York.

The buzzer rang, and Stella ran to get the door, feeling bad that Lenny had to do so much for her. Well, she couldn't have stopped him if she'd tried. He'd been looking out for her since he'd heard about the divorce.

"Ms. Spencer, it's Linda Carlton."

"Cool, send her up. Thanks, Len."

This was the final step. She was on her way. Stella tried to feel excited, but there was still that lump of grief and loss in the pit of her stomach. Funny how Sheikh Bashir had hit her as hard as Robert had. One weekend versus seven years of marriage; yet she would be hard pressed to decide which one had hurt her more.

It just takes time, Stella.

Stella was more than a little relieved when she heard the knock on her door. Being alone with her thoughts was kind of dangerous.

"Hi, Linda. Thanks for making it on such short notice," Stella said, opening the door wide.

Linda Carlton waltzed right in, her eyes big as dinner plates as she took in the tasteful designer furnishings, spacious rooms, high ceilings, and pre-war details.

"This place," she said, turning to look back at Stella, "is *amazing*. Even better than I thought when you described it over the phone."

"Thanks. Wish I could take credit for it."

"Well, I know the building. The address will sell it, no problem. Did you have a ballpark figure in mind, or…?"

Stella set her jaw. "I'm a motivated seller."

The real estate agent looked at her. "I'm sorry, hon, I have to ask…"

"Divorce."

Keep it simple. No one needs to hear the details of your dumb life.

Linda Carlton was obviously practiced at just this sort of situation. She looked genuinely sympathetic. "I get it, hon, I really do. You know I got the shaft after fifteen years?"

"I'm sorry," Stella said.

"Don't be. Screwed him out of the condo." Linda had started busily making notes, and was inspecting the moldings like a trained appraiser. "A classic six, this address? Honey, you'll be fine. The biggest issue I see is getting a sale past the co-op board, but I've worked with them before. We'll get it done, don't worry."

Stella was surprised at how relieved she felt. It was as if someone had just told her that the last cord tying her to her old life would be easy to cut.

"Thank you," she said with real gratitude, collapsing into one of Robert's expensive designer chairs. He'd gotten upset every time someone had sat in them. What else were you supposed to do with chairs? "You have my attorney's contact info, right?"

"Are you leaving town?"

Stella nodded. It sounded good already. "I don't think I'll stay more than a few days. Might even leave tonight, if I feel like it. I still have some settlement money, so I might just...wait it out in a hotel somewhere, 'til the apartment sells, you know?"

After that, it would be easy. She could buy a house out west with the cash from the apartment and still have enough left over to be comfortable, even if it sold for a rock-bottom price. She could find a place to work with people at the end of life, people who didn't want to be alone. Maybe a hospice. All on her own terms.

Linda looked up from her notepad. "Men are such bastards, aren't they?"

Stella sighed, and scooped up another bite of cookie dough. "Yes," she said. "Yes, they are."

And maybe if I say it often enough, I'll start to believe it.

But Stella's gloomy thoughts were interrupted by the buzzer from downstairs for a second time. Maybe Lenny was as telepathic as Sheikh Bashir had been. The thought made her smile a little, just before it made her sad again. *Buck up, Stella.*

"What's up, Len?" she said into the speaker box. She wasn't expecting anyone besides Linda Carlton.

"Sorry to bother you, Ms. Spencer, but they say they're calling from a hospital, and you're the only emergency contact they could get a hold of."

"What? For who?"

"A Ms. Kincaid."

Stella's blood froze. How could she be the emergency contact for Ms. Kincaid? The only way that was possible was if the Sheikh had added her. Would he do that? It was true that she'd had a rapport with Ms. Kincaid, but a rapport was a far cry from an emergency contact. And why would he entrust her with something like that if he were just planning on...

No, don't think it.

None of it made sense. But whether it made sense or not wasn't the priority. Ms. Kincaid was.

"Did they say what was wrong? Or where she was?"

"They left an address."

"Tell them I'll be right there."

It was amazing how quickly you could run out the door when you'd already decided that you had no attachments to the place where you were. Stella just grabbed her keys, told Linda to let herself out, and run out the door. She'd taken the address from Lenny, and, as luck would have it, there was a yellow cab waiting right outside the building.

Perfect.

"Carthage House, on Kraft, up in Westchester," she said. "I'll pay extra for the trip on top of the fare; I know it's way out of the city."

In retrospect, she realized that she should have been suspicious when the cabbie didn't object. It was at least thirty minutes out of Manhattan, plus another thirty minutes where he wouldn't be able to pick up any extra fares on the way back. But, as it turned out, the cabbie wasn't particularly worried about that.

Stella didn't think anything was wrong until the cab turned toward the park.

"Shouldn't you take the FDR?" she'd said.

No answer.

But she didn't get really worried until the cab pulled onto one of the side streets, just off Fifth Avenue, and into one of the few working garages in all of Manhattan. It was attached to an old, beautiful limestone townhouse.

The cab rolled to a stop in the gloom of the garage, and they sat in silence. Stella was too afraid to speak. Finally the cabbie cleared his throat.

"Please get out of the car, miss."

"I asked you to take me to Westchester."

"Someone else paid me a lot of money to take you here instead," he said, turning around with a baleful expression. "I got kids, miss. And he seemed like a nice man. You give him another chance, yeah?"

Stella closed her eyes and tried to think calm thoughts. This was...

Nope. No calm thoughts.

"No tip," she said, and slammed the door as she got out of the car. The cabbie peeled out of the garage as fast as he could, and the motorized garage doors closed quickly behind him.

Now she really was trapped. Well, not for

long. She did not have to take this. This was twenty-first century America, not some crazy tribal kingdom from the Dark Ages. She moved purposefully towards the garage doors, her heart pattering in her chest, telling herself that she'd be able to open them, no problem, of course she would, and she'd just find another cab and go back to her plans...

She was only a few steps from the door when an iron arm encircled her waist.

"No," that deep, rumbling voice said.

"Let go of me!" she screamed, fury and grief and hurt overtaking her as she beat fruitlessly at the arm that held her fast. He lifted her effortlessly, and though she kicked hard as he flipped her around and slung her over his shoulder, it was to no avail. He held her pinned and helpless as she battered his back with her tiny fists.

"You *bastard!* Let go of me!"

"Not until you promise to listen," he said. "And be reasonable."

She still hadn't seen his face.

She stopped fighting as he carried her through a servant's entrance and up a flight of narrow stairs to one of the grand areas of the house, but she definitely wasn't going to promise to be 'reasonable.' As far as she was concerned, her reaction *was* perfectly reasonable.

Well, part of her reaction, anyway. The

other part, where her body hummed everywhere he touched her, and the part where she felt herself getting wet when he restrained her...

That was less reasonable.

"You can't treat someone like this," she said into his back, wondering where the hell he was taking her.

"I can do whatever I want," he said mildly. "I own you, remember? The transaction has not been completed."

She gritted her teeth. Now he really *was* a bastard.

"So you got my letter, then."

"It wasn't a letter. It was a check in an envelope."

"*Your* check."

They'd entered another room now; this one had what looked like traditional Arab or Bedouin furnishings: tapestries, ottomans, rugs, lamps. Suddenly Stella was pitched backward. She landed on something soft, and bounced slightly: a bed.

And there was Sheikh Bashir, standing over her, eyes glowing. He looked amazing in a crisp white shirt, his hair loose, his shoulders bulging.

"*Listen*," she began angrily, and tried to scoot off of the bed. Sheikh Bashir caught her wrists easily.

"No, no, Stella," he said firmly, dragging

her to the head of the bed. "First, you will listen."

"What do you think you're doing?"

But Stella could plainly see what he was doing; she just couldn't believe it. He'd had some sort of silk scarves within reach of the bed, and was lashing her wrists to the headboard.

He ignored her question, but caught her ankle when she tried to kick him. "Do you want me to tie your legs, as well?" he asked, eyebrows raised. He looked at the posts of the large bed, so wide apart. "That could be interesting, indeed."

Stella blushed. Again, she had to remember to remain angry while her body screamed for him. She hadn't been able to forget what it had felt like to have him inside her. She doubted she ever would.

Sheikh Bashir looked at her with that penetrating stare, and an evil smile played across his lips. "It's not time for that yet, Stella," he said. "First, we talk."

Oh, that is just not fair.

"Screw you, Sheikh. Seriously."

He burst out laughing, which, obviously, infuriated her. He said, "That can be arranged. But first I would like to tell you about my week. Then you can tell me about yours. And then we can discuss how we'll spend the rest of the day."

Stella fumed silently. She couldn't move, but she wouldn't give him the satisfaction of her acknowledgement. She watched as he moved to the enormous multi-paned windows and drew the heavy, dark red curtains, giving the room an intimate, secluded feel. *He wants me to forget about the rest of the world*, she thought.

Well, he was in luck. It was damned hard to think about anything else with Sheikh Bashir standing in front of her. He rolled up the cuffs of that crisp white shirt to expose his dark, muscled forearms, and she almost groaned. It was cruelly unfair.

"Stella," he said seriously. "Will you listen?"

"Do I have much choice?"

His lips curled up at the edges. "No, I suppose you don't."

He climbed up on the bed and grabbed hold of her ankles, easily maneuvering himself between her legs, and held her in place. "But just to make sure," he said.

He certainly had her attention. She tried to ignore the swelling pulse between her legs and the aching awareness in her breasts, and glared at him. He suddenly looked very serious.

"Stella, I did not mean to leave you. I never, ever meant to leave you. It was a terrible mistake, one that I will…" He stopped himself, as though he was unsure of what he had almost said.

That's not like him, she thought. *That's not like*

him at all.

"I was tricked," he said, breathing out. "Do you remember Creighton?"

"How could I forget? You introduce me to such lovely people."

Sheikh Bashir's eyes flashed. If they were still lovers, if it had been only a few days before this, Stella was sure that that remark would have earned her some punishment. Part of her hoped it still would.

Get a grip, Stella! Think with your brain!

"Be that as it may," he continued, "Creighton did not forget about his humiliation at my hand, and on your behalf. His family is very powerful, and very connected — especially locally. He used those connections to dupe an unsuspecting police captain into harassing me. The police arrived at the hotel and claimed to have a warrant for your arrest."

Fear settled in Stella's chest. It was a reflexive reaction. She'd always been on the honor roll; she'd always been the one to raise her hand for every question; she'd never even gotten a freaking parking ticket. A warrant? For her?

"It was a ruse, Stella," Sheikh Bashir said, and brushed his hand against her cheek.

His touch was electrifying. She turned her face toward his hand without thinking, hungry for more, then blinked back frustrated tears.

"Damn you," she whispered.

"They arrested me when I went downstairs to inform them of their error," he said gently, but refused to take his hand away. Instead, he caressed her cheek. "I did not have any identification with me to prove my diplomatic immunity, and the deceived officers conveniently lost my paperwork several times. I was in jail until this morning."

Stella's anger and grief gave way, suddenly, to a torrent of worry. In jail? For three days? All alone, and with no one who knew he was there?

"Are you ok?" she asked. "Did anything...I mean, are you...?"

"I'm fine, Stella," Sheikh Bashir said, his eyes soft. "Nothing like that could hurt me. It was nothing, compared to..."

He seemed to lose his words then, and a small vein in his throat began to throb. Sheikh Bashir cleared his throat.

"I thought only of you, Stella. I thought of the things I did not have a chance to say to you, and I thought of how I must have hurt you, and it was a pain unlike anything I've ever experienced, Stella, and I never want to experience it ever again. It was..."

He shook his head then, and she only wanted to help, to make him feel better. It wasn't his fault.

"You don't have to feel bad for me," she

said. "It was a misunderstanding."

His jaw clenched. "Do not talk about yourself like that."

"What?"

"You are not an object of pity. You are..." He gripped the back of her head and leaned forward suddenly, his face hovering right above hers. "You are beloved."

He kissed her deeply, his whole body sinking into hers, his lips melting her mouth until she yearned for the rest of the barriers between them to simply disappear.

"How do you always know what I'm thinking?" she asked as he moved to her neck. He felt so, so good against her body, and she only wanted more of him, and yet certain thoughts were pressing insistently against her brain. "Wait, how did you know where I lived?"

He stopped and sighed.

"And why did you leave me that check?" she demanded, and the memory of it was enough to bring tears back to her eyes. She had to be careful with this man. He made her body lie to her.

Sheikh Bashir sat up, his full, broad torso blocking out what little light there was in the room. Even with all the unanswered questions, Stella missed the feeling of his weight on top of her. The movement of her hips betrayed her thoughts, and she hated herself a little bit for that. He put his hands on the sides of her hips, gripping them, and that...did not help.

"No, you are right," he said. "A full explanation is warranted. Ms. Kincaid is fine. I used her abominably, as part of my own ruse to get you here, but I feel she would approve if I could make her understand. I knew where you lived because I commissioned a report on you from the security firm I keep on retainer. It is standard practice for a man in my position, though I understand if you feel violated. If it will help, I will commission a report on myself, for your eyes only."

"Violated?" The word did not make her think of investigative reports. She was getting distracted again. She shook her head and said, "What about the check? Why—"

"That damned check," he said vehemently. "I have never been that stupid in my entire life—you must believe me. I made it out at the beginning of the weekend, and simply forgot."

"But why...in the first place..." she said quietly. She'd wondered the whole time why he would insist on paying anyone for what he had apparently wanted. It hadn't made sense to her. He'd spent the whole weekend thinking about her pleasure, her well-being, her feelings, and then he had to distance himself from all of it with an absurd amount of money.

Now the Sheikh grabbed her by the chin and looked directly into her eyes. "Because I was a coward, too, Stella. I planned on a weekend I could walk away from without any attachments, because I was afraid of becoming attached."

"Everyone's afraid." Stella said. She wished she could comfort him, but he shook his head bitterly.

"There is no excuse for it. You asked how I always seem to know what you are thinking? Because someone hurt me once by lying to me. A woman. She was...she was the reason I ended my friendship with Mark Kincaid, because he warned me and I chose this woman over a loyal friend. I swore that no one would ever deceive me again. I had studied the face-reading techniques of Paul Eckman and others, for professional and political reasons, given my family's position, but after Vanessa deceived me with another man, I devoted myself to the practice utterly. It was—is—all about control. I was simply afraid, Stella," he concluded. "And I was right to be. I think I've loved you from the first moment I saw you."

It was like all the air left the room at once, and the vacuum it left behind pulled the words from her against her will.

"I love you, too," she blurted out. Had she even admitted that to herself before now?

Did it matter?

Sheikh Bashir looked just as taken aback as Stella felt. "I will do everything in my power to make a life you want," he said. "A charity, your own organization, for the abandoned elderly. Houses, as many as — "

"I want you," she whispered.

The Sheikh inhaled deeply, his whole body seeming to expand. Then his hand snaked out and, in one motion, all the buttons of her blouse snapped open.

"I did not kidnap you for conversation," he said, eyes glinting. He grabbed her breasts and raked his hands down the length of her body, unzipping her jeans and pulling them off in one impressive motion. He frowned at her panties, then ripped them off.

"Spread for me," he said. "My love."

Stella did.

ABOUT THE AUTHOR

Chloe Cox writes happily from both coasts and parts of the world exotic. You can visit her at chloecoxwrites.com.

4459364R00159

Made in the USA
San Bernardino, CA
21 September 2013